SHOW ME

Janet Dailey

Show Me

G.K. Hall & Co. • **Chivers Press**
Thorndike, Maine USA Bath, England

This Large Print edition is published by G.K. Hall & Co., USA and by Chivers Press, England.

Published in 2000 in the U.S. by arrangement with Richard Curtis Associates, Inc.

Published in 2000 in the U.K. by arrangement with the author.

U.S.   Hardcover 0-7838-9111-3 (Core Series Edition)
U.K.   Hardcover 0-7540-4269-3 (Chivers Large Print)
U.K.   Softcover   0-7540-4270-7 (Camden Large Print)

The text of this Large Print edition is unabridged.
Other aspects of the book may vary from the original edition.

Set in 16 pt. Plantin by Anne Bradeen.

Printed in the United States on permanent paper.

British Library Cataloguing-in-Publication Data available

Library of Congress Cataloging-in-Publication Data

Dailey, Janet.
    Show me / Janet Dailey.
        p. cm.
    ISBN 0-7838-9111-3 (lg. print : hc : alk. paper)
    1. Missouri — Fiction. 2. Large type books.   I. Title.
PS3554.A29 S48 2000
    813′.54—dc21
                                                    00-031959

Show Me

CHAPTER ONE

The asphalt road snaked along the ridge, writhing and slithering its way towards Dewey Bald. Here and there the trees fell away to allow a panoramic glimpse of the Ozark Mountains of Missouri. The sylvan hillsides were coloured in myriad spring greens, from the deep hues of the cedars all the way to the pale greens of newly budding trees, an array as spectacular as autumn's bold splashes. The burgeoning world was highlighted by the mauve shades of the redbud tree and the symbolic white blossoms of the flowering dogwood, while the rock-strewn ground burst forth with an explosion of wild spring flowers.

'Can we stop at Sammy's Lookout?'

The small, questioning voice drew Tanya Lassiter's wandering gaze away from the road and scenery ahead of them. Her mouth curved into a smile as she gazed at the silently pleading blue eyes staring so earnestly back at her. Baby-fine brown hair covered his forehead, softening the effect of his pointed chin. No one else could have a little boy as beautiful and intelligent as her John, Tanya thought to herself with a warm glow of satisfaction. At seven, he was as impish and happy and curious as anyone would want their child to be. Who could remain immune to the entreaty of those trusting eyes that invariably reminded her of the clear blue colour of warm summer skies — so unlike Jake's, his father, whose eyes held the metallic sheen of blue steel.

'Can we?' John repeated.

'We can for a little while,' Tanya agreed. Her lips had tightened fractionally and she forced them to relax. 'But Grandmother will have supper for us, so we can't stay too long.'

There was no enthusiastic response from John, causing Tanya to glance wonderingly at his averted head. His thoughtful pose, as he gazed out the side window of the station wagon, arched one of her delicate brows before it settled back into place. Whatever was troubling John would soon be confided to her once he had methodically thought it through on his own.

Tanya was busy locking the car doors while John waited with thinly disguised impatience a few feet away from where the wagon was parked along the road. The pullover sweater vest matched the thin maroon stripe in her slacks with the complementing background of cream yellow in her long-sleeved blouse. Sliding out from behind the wheel and closing the door, she smoothed her hair into its band and hurried to join the slender boy in his light blue windbreaker and crisp blue jeans.

Together they traversed the few hundred yards

back to the big grey stone overlooking Mutton Hollow and the Trail That Was Nobody Knows How Old. They made a striking pair, one tall, lithe and feminine, the other exhibiting the vitality of youth in a masculine miniature. While John made straight for the large, slate-grey rock, Tanya sought the seclusion of a small boulder farther up the hillside. It denied her the view of the valley, but it hid her from the sight of passing motorists on the road just below. The traffic was mostly local now. The tourist jam would come with the summer sun.

The boy stood on the rock, gazing out over the scenery, his legs spread apart in a proud stance with his hands on his hips. In some ways, John was like herself. On the surface he possessed an outgoing personality, gregarious, fun-loving and always curious, but he, like Tanya, had those moments when he enjoyed being alone with his own thoughts. There were times when she felt that at seven years old John was too serious, too contemplative and too much in the company of adults, but with children his own age in school, there was never any reserve or any inability to relate to his peers. So she had marked her worry off to an over-abundance of conscience.

Leaning back against the slanting hillside, Tanya watched the sun slowly settling on the western slopes. The bright plumage of a male robin darted in front of her as he flew in attendance on his chosen mate. A surging ache rose from deep inside, shooting through her limbs

9

until she wanted to hug her arms about her to ward off the pain. This was the natural mating season and Tanya recognized the inexplicable longing inside was the same desire for a mate of her own. She was a woman, a twenty-six-year-old female of her species, in need of a male to love. The simplest and oldest truth of life.

There was no vanity in recognizing her own beauty. And Tanya was beautiful. Long hair that hesitated between light brown and blonde with occasional natural streaks of shimmering honey was brushed straight back from her smooth fore-head in a leonine style that was vastly becoming to her perfect features. There was a classic lift to her cheekbones and nose, and a warm, sensuous mouth that could transform the cool, marble beauty of her face into enticing witchery with a smile. But it was her tawny, gold-flecked eyes that kept the shutters closed on the smouldering passions that lay below the surface.

Nothing remained of the haunted, slightly vengeful young girl who had come to these hills over seven years ago with a boy child in her arms. The influence and example of her mother-in-law, Julia Lassiter, had erased the schoolgirl image and replaced it with a poised, sophisticated young woman. Only one thing remained, Tanya thought with carefully nurtured bitterness, and that was her loathing of Jake Lassiter, the man whose name she bore. The only saving grace of her marriage had been that she had John. He belonged to her and could never be taken away — as long as she remained married to Jake.

'Mother?'

The lids that had drifted down over her burnished tan eyes fluttered open. Tanya straightened to sit erectly as John settled on the ground beside her, a tanned hand plucking at the sprouting grass.

'Yes, John?' Tanya curled her arms around her knees and waited.

'Do I really have a father?'

Only for a second did the shock of his question register on her face. 'Of course you do.' Her heart thudded a little louder in her chest, but there was no other outward sign that his words had disconcerted her.

'I mean, is he really alive?' This time the troubled blue eyes stared into her face, earnest and searching.

'Yes, he's alive. You yourself have brought his letters from home from the mailbox. Whatever made you think that he wasn't?' Tanya tried to laugh lightly, but it came out shrill and without amusement.

'Danny Gilbert said he must be dead or in prison or he'd come home. He isn't in prison, is he?'

'No, darling, he isn't in prison. He's somewhere in Africa right now.' Her arm went around the slim shoulders, drawing the tense boy against her body, afraid he would see that she had no wish to talk about Jake Lassiter. 'He works for your grandfather, remember? And there's a big dam or bridge or something being built over there and your grandfather's company is supervising the work. Your father is over there making sure it's done right.'

'But why doesn't he ever come home? And why don't we ever go to visit him? Doesn't he want to see us?' The silky brown head pulled away from the hand that was stroking it to gaze in confusion at the frown creasing Tanya's forehead.

'He will come home some day,' she attempted to reassure him, but the very ambiguousness of her answer defeated her. 'He's very busy.'

'Everybody gets vacations. Why can't he take a vacation and come visit us?'

'He did do that once.' Not daring to add that Jake had ostensibly come home for a month's stay and had left after a week.

'I was a baby.' The child rebuffed her answer in a disgruntled tone. 'Three years old, Grandmother said. I don't remember him at all.'

'Have . . . have you discussed this with your grandmother?' Tanya asked hesitantly. One more black mark would go against Tanya in her mother-in-law's book if he had.

'No.' John lifted his shoulders in an expressive little shrug. 'I only asked her how old I was when I got that ivory statue of an elephant. You told me my father brought it home to me as a present.'

Yes, Tanya remembered his question several days before, but had given it no special significance. A tiny sigh of relief escaped her lips.

'Can we visit him this summer after school is finished?'

'It . . . Your fa . . .' She stumbled desperately to find a way of refusing the request without adding more fuel to John's growing opinion that his father wanted nothing to do with him. It was there in the defeated dullness of his eyes. 'The political situation over there isn't such that we can.'

'I knew you'd say something like that.' The pseudo-adult bitterness in his voice lashed out at her with the smarting flick of a whip.

'Perhaps,' Tanya swallowed nervously, hating the suggestion that was forming on her lips, 'we could write a letter to your father tonight and see if he could arrange to come home for a couple of weeks this summer.'

A small hand brushed the silken brown hair away from his forehead as John turned to stare into her face, a half-hopeful expression in his eyes. Unwillingly, her gaze strayed to the crooked little finger, the mark that from birth had affirmed his right to the Lassiter name.

'Do you think he would come?' he asked.

Secretly she hoped he wouldn't, but the silent prayer that Jake would refuse died as she gazed into the boy's face. 'If it's at all possible, I'm sure he will, especially if you write to ask him.' Tanya had never tried to encourage any correspondence between father and son, unwilling to share John's love with the man she loathed. Only at

Christmas time and birthdays did she prompt John to send a thank-you note for the packages that dutifully arrived in the mails.

'We'd better get home.' John hopped to his feet, a wide beaming smile splitting his face.

'John, just because we write your father,' Tanya spoke quietly several minutes later as she turned the station wagon onto the lake road leading home, 'there's no guarantee that he'll be able to come back to the States.'

'I know. But he will come, I know he will!' The determination in the small boy's voice reminded her how strong the bond was between a father and son. Much as she wanted to ignore her husband's existence, for John's sake she couldn't. 'Besides,' John went on, 'I've been thinking that maybe he thinks I don't care about him. If he knows how much I want to see him, he'll come home. I'm sure of it.'

'Well, perhaps if not this summer, he might be able to come in the fall or even at Christmas time. Don't build your hopes up too high, John. He may not be able to get away.'

'I wish he could come home now so Danny Gilbert could see that I really do have a father and that he really has been in Africa.' He glanced earnestly at her. 'Can we write that letter right after supper?'

'Yes, right after supper,' Tanya promised with a little sinking of her heart.

'And we'll send it airmail so he'll get it right away?'

'Yes, we'll send it airmail,' she nodded reluctantly.

'Uncle Patrick's car is in the drive,' John announced gaily at the sight of the silver El Dorado parked in front of the ultra-modern ranch-style home. 'It's been ages since he's been here.'

'Only a little over a week,' she corrected, her eyes sparkling too, at the sight of the familiar car.

Patrick Raines wasn't truly John's uncle, although he had called him that ever since he could talk. Now that Tanya's father-in-law, J. D. Lassiter, had gone into semi-retirement, going to his firm's office in Springfield only two or three times a week, Patrick Raines was head of the engineering firm in all but name. It was a feeling Tanya had that J.D. was keeping his hand in the operation until Jake returned to the States, at which time he would turn it over to his only living son. It had been her father-in-law's persuasion that had brought Jake home for an abortive stay four years ago. But no one had been immune to the chilling and hostile atmosphere that had surrounded Jake and Tanya. She hadn't been able to carry on a civil conversation with him, let alone be comfortable in the same room with him.

As she and young John walked on to the highly polished tiled floor of the foyer, Tanya felt her heart skipping a beat at the sound of Patrick's rich voice in the next room. John went dashing ahead of her, calling out a greeting to his grandparents and to the dark handsome man just

15

coming into Tanya's sight. Her mouth curved into a welcoming smile under the warm regard of Patrick Raines.

'It's good to see you again, Patrick.' Her hand reached out naturally for his, enjoying the firm, lingering touch that reinforced the glow in his brown eyes. 'John commented when he saw your car that you hadn't been here for ages.'

'Then you did miss me while I was out of town,' his resonant voice declared with satisfaction.

Tanya was about to seize on his statement, having no knowledge that he had been away, when her mother-in-law broke into the conversation. 'We were beginning to give you two up for lost. Where did you and Johnny wander off to?' Only Julia Lassiter ever called John Johnny, and Tanya was sure her mother-in-law did it because Julia knew how it irritated her.

'We went on a little side trip that took longer than we expected,' she replied calmly, turning towards the woman firmly holding John's hand. Her gold-flecked eyes flickered over the aristocratic face with its framework of professionally dyed blue-grey hair, knowing Julia's avarice for a detailed account of their every movement. 'Is dinner ready?'

'We were just finishing our sherry before going in,' J.D. announced, unfolding his tall form from the velvet sofa and rising to his feet, an imposing figure of a man, like his son.

'Give us a few minutes to freshen up and we'll

be down.' Tanya held out her hand for John and flashed a smile aimed generally at the trio, but resting a shade longer on Patrick.

In record time, she changed out of her slacks and blouse and into a well cut shirtwaister dress, the paisley pattern in carnelian red and rich navy blue. The confining hairband was removed and her tawny brown hair was brushed straight back from her forehead to fall around her long slim neck and shoulders to curl at the ends. The very simplicity of the hairstyle and dress bespoke sophistication and poise.

Tanya went immediately to the kitchen, knowing full well that Julia expected her to be there. The Lassiters could afford a maid or a cook or a gardener, but Julia Lassiter's home was her private castle. The work was either done by herself or under her watchful eye. The woman was perfect, Tanya decided grimly. There was nothing she couldn't do as well as the best and better than the average. Her meals were a gourmet's dream, but with a sufficient touch of the commonplace to satisfy her husband's palate. The house was always immaculately clean with never a smidgeon of dust hiding in any forgotten corner or almost inaccessible nook. The garden, an extensive and imaginative piece of work, was tended only by Julia, although she graciously allowed Tanya or her husband to do the more mundane chores of mowing the expensive lawn area. And her person she kept elegantly groomed, never a hair out of place, no smudging of lipstick; a loose button was unthinkable; and her slips never peeped out beneath the hem of a dress.

There was ample evidence Julia was not only a perfect wife and housekeeper, but also a mother. Never once did she question Jake about the gauche young girl he had brought home as his wife, nor commented on the baby boy he had identified as his son. Without the flicker of an eyebrow, she had carried out Jake's wishes that he and Tanya have separate rooms. Not one word of recrimination had been directed at Tanya when her son had left within a few days of bringing his bride home, nor in the years that followed when he stayed away. Yet Tanya had the distinct feeling that she was only tolerated in Julia's home because of John, who had become the centre of Julia's universe. Tanya always heard an underlying tone of acidity in her mother-in-law's voice whenever it was directed at her, and after all these years in the same house together, never once had there been a hint of affection or friendship to penetrate the cool reserve of Julia's grey-blue eyes.

Jake's father, J. D. Lassiter, was different altogether. Tanya had once said with biting cynicism that Jake could charm the fangs away from a cobra, and after meeting J.D., she knew this ability had been gained from his father. J.D. was more honest and open with his feelings. When she had first come to his home with little John, he had been openly sceptical of her and decidedly disapproving of his son's marriage to her. J. D. Lassiter was an autocrat and a powerful one — there was never any doubt about that. A shrewd businessman, a recognized expert in his field, and a keen judge of character, he had observed her transformation from an unworldly young girl barely out of school to a sophisticated young lady.

Gradually his thinly veiled disapproval of her had changed to respect and admiration. A quiet hand of friendship had been extended to Tanya almost five years ago. Although there never had been any questions from J.D. about her relationship with Jake, she sensed that he knew the circumstances that had surrounded their marriage. Of course, he couldn't know the whole truth. That secret was hers alone and she guarded it tenaciously, just as she guarded John. Yet it was her father-in-law's droll wit and affection that had made it bearable to remain. But she would have gone through any hell that would have given John a name, a family and a future.

Julia already had the first course of their evening meal on the table when Tanya arrived in the kitchen. Her apology for arriving too late to help was drowned out by her mother-in-law's announcement that dinner was to be served. John was already taking his seat next to his grandmother as J.D. held the chair out on his right for Tanya. She smiled across the table at the square-jawed man sitting opposite her, a warmth pervading her at his answering smile.

'You look ravishing in that dress, but then you would no matter what you wore,' Patrick remarked.

'You're very generous, but a woman likes to hear those things, no matter how untrue they may be.' Her voice was warmly polite as her gaze rested briefly on his strong resilient features and his darkly curling hair with a premature touch of grey around the temples.

That undercurrent of electricity was flowing between them, its tingling existence a nearly tangible thing that couldn't be ignored. The Lassiters entertained the executives of their company quite often and it had become an accepted thing that Patrick and Tanya should be paired together automatically. Her husband was in Africa for an indefinite period and Patrick Raines had been divorced for three years with his ex-wife remarried. Tanya tried to check the leaping of her senses whenever his dark gaze strayed to her, nullifying her reaction with the reminder that Patrick was the only eligible male she knew, and it was consistent with her romantic, secretly passionate nature to weave fantasies about a man as handsome and charming as Patrick.

The few times they had been alone together, not an indiscreet word had been uttered, yet Tanya knew theirs was not a friendship between two people. They were both too aware of each other as members of the opposite sex, but Tanya's old-fashioned morals wouldn't allow her to disregard the diamond wedding ring on her finger and her vows of fidelity, regardless of the manner of man she had given them to.

'Tell me,' picking up her soup spoon and averting her gaze from his face, 'where your travels took you to this time, Patrick. I had no idea you were going on a trip.'

'It was a spur-of-the moment journey to Scotland for the company,' a tiny pause, 'with a major side trip to South Africa.'

There was a hairline fracture in Tanya's poise, so minute that only J.D. noticed it, his iron-dark head inclining towards his wife at the other end of the table.

'Mother doesn't allow business talk at the table — a rule of the house, Patrick. As if anything could detract a man from your onion soup, Mother. It's superb as usual.' His fulsome compliment was intended to tactfully shift the conversation.

'Did you say you went to Africa, Uncle Patrick?' John piped up, a suppressed excitement in his voice.

'John!' Tanya softened the sharp reprimand in her voice. 'You heard your grandfather. Wait until after we've eaten.'

'Right.' He lowered his brown head to gaze into his soup cup and Tanya knew his sudden interest in his father would erupt the minute the dessert dishes were cleared. She wasn't quite ready to acknowledge to the rest of the family her intentions to write Jake asking him to come home.

A quick glance at Julia Lassiter's averted gaze indicated the source of the slight chill in the air. Tanya sighed inwardly, guessing that she must have thought the reprimand uncalled-for when John was only going to inquire about his father. She had to admit to herself that it probably was, but she didn't want Jake's name spoiling her dinner as it undoubtedly would.

'Before you and John arrived tonight,' J.D. had picked up the conversation again with the adroitness of an expert at table talk, 'we were discussing the possibilities of having a small dinner party to celebrate our thirty-fifth wedding anniversary on the eighth of May.'

'I think that's an excellent idea,' Tanya agreed.

'I'm glad you think so,' J.D. nodded with a twinkle. 'Mother thought it would be in bad taste to initiate a party on behalf of our own anniversary. Normally she seeks any excuse to entertain.'

'Weather permitting, Julia, we could have it out on the patio. All your spring flowers would be blooming by then and it would be ideal,' Tanya suggested, noticing the grudging agreement gleaming in her mother-in-law's eyes.

'And you could do some of that baked trout that I like so well,' J.D. interposed, 'and serve the meal buffet style.'

The topics of guests, food, and decorations for the proposed party dominated the conversation through the salad course, the exquisitely prepared standing rib roast and the crême-dementhe parfait. The telephone rang just as Julia was about to serve their after-dinner coffee in the living room, and Tanya was delegated to pour while her mother-in-law went to answer it. The caller wanted to speak to J.D., which left Tanya and Patrick alone together as little John had dashed off to his room on some secret errand.

'Patrick —' Tanya nervously cupped her hands around the delicate china receptacle, tossing her tawny brown hair over her shoulder with a flick of her head, 'when you were in Africa — did you see Jake?'

A lightning quick glance was darted at her as he leaned against the back of the sofa. 'Yes, yes, I did.' His dark gaze showed the same intense interest in the black liquid in his cup as she did.

'The project he's working on, how is it coming along?' It was cheating, she knew, to try to determine what the chances were that Jake might take her up on the invitation she was about to issue that he return home, but she had to know.

'Which one?' Patrick asked dryly. 'The one he's finishing or the one that's just starting?'

Relief raced through her and unknowingly she sighed. 'I didn't know he was working on two different projects. It must keep him very busy.'

'Lonnie Danvers is a very capable assistant, but Jake still has to do a lot of commuting between sites, at least for the time being.'

Tanya was glad of Julia's return. It saved her from explaining the reason for her questions, and the curious glint in Patrick's eyes had indicated that he was about to ask it. J.D. entered the room within seconds of his wife, sent her a quick smile of apology, and launched into a brief business discussion with Patrick that excluded the two women.

As Julia seemed preoccupied with some thoughts of her own, Tanya took the opportunity to study the dark-haired man sitting opposite her now that the prospect of Jake's returning to the States seemed so remote. During the years she had lived with her in-laws, she had noticed the way so many people kowtowed to the Lassiters' wealth and power. One of the first things she had admired about Patrick Raines was his refusal to give lip service to J. D. Lassiter. He was his own man and never hesitated to voice an objection and stick with it if his views didn't match those of the firm's owner. Yet Patrick wasn't so independent that he wouldn't seek the older man's advice and experience if he felt he needed it. There was more than just charm and intelligence behind the handsome facade that drew Tanya.

A small hand touched her shoulder. She glanced up into a pair of clear blue eyes.

'Can we go and do it now, Mom?' His oblique request only made sense to Tanya.

'Go and do what, dear?' Julia inserted, her slightly raised voice drawing the attention of the two men.

'I'm going to write my father a letter asking him to come home on his vacation.' His young voice was filled with importance.

Tanya studied the proud tilt of his head, a rosy hue colouring her cheeks as she felt the eyes in the room looking at her. Patrick had only guessed at her animosity towards her husband, but his parents knew of its existence. Their curiosity about her reaction to John's announcement weighted the silence.

'I think that's an excellent idea, Johnny,' Julia Lassiter said firmly, the tone of her voice daring Tanya to disagree.

The slight flush receded as Tanya turned her cool amber gaze towards her mother-in-law, her marble smooth features composed. 'So do I, Julia,' she agreed with freezing calm, 'which is why I suggested it to John.'

She wanted no further discussion on the matter, no pseudo-innocent delving by Julia into her motives or even by J.D., so she rose from her chair, resting a hand on John's slim shoulders as she guided him out of the living room.

'You want to write the letter, don't you?' the boy asked hesitantly when they had arrived in the alcove off Tanya's bedroom.

'Yes, John,' she smiled down at him, swallowing the distaste in her mouth the words caused. From what Patrick had said, there was little chance that Jake would come or could come. A twinge of guilt raced through her as she forced herself to be cheerful. 'We'll both write to him.'

John fumbled in his shirt pocket, finally withdrawing a photograph which he handed to her. 'I thought we could send along this picture Grandfather took when I got my new bike . . . so Father will know what I look like.'

John wasn't the only one in the picture. Tanya was there too, laughing into the camera, her dark blonde hair ruffled by the wind and looking every inch a sophisticated, well-bred member of society, and hardly the mother of the young boy astride the bicycle.

'He has your school pictures, John,' she reminded him gently, strangely unwilling to send the photograph in her hand.

'But they don't look like me and I had a tooth missing,' he protested. 'Please, can't we send it?'

With that pair of pleading blue eyes looking at her, Tanya knew she would always give in. A part of her admitted, however reluctantly, that John was getting to the age where he needed the strong guiding hand of a man, something that was his father's responsibility.

An hour later the feelings of guilt that she had deprived John of his father had subsided as she sealed the envelope containing the letters from John and herself. His was a heart-tugging, scrawling message politely inquiring if his father could come home this summer. Hers was as simple, stating John's sudden doubts that he really had a father and impersonally adding that perhaps Jake should come home for a few weeks if his work would permit it. With the airmail stamp on the envelope, Tanya felt the pinpricks of her conscience had been assuaged. She

26

loathed Jake Lassiter for the things he had done in the past, but for John's sake she would tolerate his presence — if Jake came. And Tanya was almost positive he wouldn't.

CHAPTER TWO

'You look beautiful, Mom,' John declared as Tanya set the portable television on top of the small desk in his bedroom.

'Do you like the dress?' A graceful pirouette sent the orange-flame chiffon of the skirt swirling about her knees. Her long, streaked tawny-blonde hair was brushed back from her forehead and behind her ears where two simple hoops of gold dangled from her lobes. 'I bought it especially for your grandparents' anniversary party tonight.'

'It's terrific. I wish I could go to the party,' he sighed.

'And think of the television programmes you'll miss. I think the movie tonight is a western,' Tanya teased.

'Is it?' His eyes lit up. John was typically boy when it came to westerns. Most other programmes bored him as he preferred to generate his own adventures.

'Some of the guests will have already arrived. You'll be all right, won't you?' she smiled.

'Sure,' he shrugged off-handedly.

'Lights out at ten o'clock,' Tanya reminded

him. 'I'll be back to make sure they are.'

'Okay, Mom,' he grinned as she lifted her hand in goodbye before stepping out of his room into the hallway.

They both knew it was an excuse to return at ten because John considered himself too old to be tucked in although neither one wanted to discontinue the nightly ritual.

The rooms of the one-storey ranch-style home that Tanya and John occupied were in a separate wing of the house, originally to be used as guest rooms with the Lassiters' master suite on the other side of the house. Now they were more or less separate apartments, minus kitchen privileges, which enabled John and Tanya to have some degree of privacy.

The structure itself, a blend of native stone and wood, was situated on the point of a finger of land jutting into Table Rock Lake. The sheltered cove of water contained a private dock and enclosed boathouse. There were no neighbours as J. D. Lassiter had purchased the adjoining land to ensure his privacy and isolation. Any invitation to the home was treated as a royal summons and was never declined, hence the houseful of guests that evening.

The doorbell rang as Tanya's heels clicked on to the tiled foyer. 'I'll answer it, Julia,' she called, hearing her mother-in-law's footsteps approaching from the kitchen. She swung the embossed wood entrance door wide, admitting Patrick Raines and the petite, dark-haired girl who accompanied him.

'Sheila, I'm so glad you could come!' Tanya exclaimed, reaching out to grasp the ringed hand of Patrick's sister. 'Your dress is divine,' she added, taking in the white eyelet lace gown that complemented the young girl's dark beauty.

'It's terribly colourless next to yours,' Sheila commented, a glint of envy and something else in her brown eyes as she made a quick and thorough appraisal of Tanya's appearance.

There was only four years' difference in their ages, Sheila being twenty-two, but Tanya never felt she was accepted by Patrick's sister. Tonight there was even a smug sort of glitter in the dark gaze that made Tanya believe her welcome for the girl should have been a bit more cool and sophisticated.

'We aren't late, are we?' Patrick enquired, his blandness overridden by the admiring expression in his eyes as they wandered over the long orange-red sleeves and the low scooped neckline of Tanya's dress.

'Not at all. The others are out on the patio.'

The foyer — Julia preferred to call it a breezeway — ran the full width of the house, culminating in sliding glass doors that opened on to the patio and the surrounding rock garden. With the lake less than a hundred yards away, there had never been a swimming pool installed. Julia Lassiter hadn't wanted it anyway for fear it would spoil the aesthetic effect of her garden.

As the trio joined the rest of the guests, J. D.

30

Lassiter immediately excused himself from the couple he was with to come forward to greet the new arrivals. Julia appeared a few minutes later, carrying a replenished tray of her hors d'oeuvres.

For the next hour and a half, Tanya was occupied answering the doorbell, helping her mother-in-law arrange the food on the buffet table, later clearing the half-consumed dishes away, and chatting with the twenty-odd couples who were attending the party. It was something of a relief when Patrick appeared with a pair of drinks in his hands and ordered her to sit down on the cushioned redwood bench and relax.

'I don't know why the Old Man doesn't have these affairs catered,' Patrick declared, leaning against the rear cushion and trailing his arm along the back near enough to Tanya's shoulders to cause a disturbance not revealed by her outward poise. 'It would be much less work for you and Julia.'

'But then the credit wouldn't be Julia's,' Tanya sighed before grimacing ruefully. 'That sounded catty! It's true, though. If this party was catered, she would still be supervising every move. It's her nature.'

'What's your nature?' he asked softly, the look in his eyes shutting out the rest of the people chattering about them.

'My nature?' She paused, gazing out past the lanterns that lit the patio to the silvery trail of moonlight on the lake. 'I would have probably invited a fourth as many people and cooked steaks on a grill.'

'Invite me to your next party,' Patrick smiled. 'It sounds delightfully intimate.'

'I will.' Tanya had to look away from the hypnotic mouth so far away and yet so incredibly close. 'It's a lovely evening, isn't it?'

'Very,' he replied, without taking his eyes off her. 'That's an excellent choice of music on the stereo.'

Tanya paused to listen, hearing the haunting strains of 'Unchained Melody' filtering softly through the steady din of voices. The melancholy tune filled her with an aching desire to be held in the warmth of a man's arms, if only for a little while.

'How many eyebrows do you think we'd raise if we danced over in that empty corner by the speakers?' Patrick asked, the dark brilliance of his sideways glance chasing over her face.

'Probably everyone's,' she breathed, wondering if she had betrayed herself by look or word.

'Let's chance it,' he suggested quietly, his hand reaching out to claim hers and draw her to her feet.

A magic spell seemed to be wrapped around them. Only Sheila looked their way, a knowing expression in her brown eyes. Tanya couldn't remember the last time she had been held in a man's arms or firmly wouldn't remember as she willingly surrendered herself to Patrick's guidance. He kept to simple steps that didn't require much concentration, so Tanya was able to imprint the feel of his firm grip on her waist, holding her as close to him as propriety would permit.

The gentle caress of his breath against her hair made her want to lay her head against his chest, but she steeled herself against it, although she did allow her hand to creep a little further along his shoulders.

'Tanya.' The softness of his voice brought her chin up so that she was gazing into his tanned face, now dangerously close to hers. That delicious sensation of being held by a man had her face aglow, especially so since she was gazing into such a handsome face.

'You're so incredibly beautiful,' he murmured. The ardent light in his eyes sent her heart tripping away. For one treacherously weak moment, she wanted to forget convention, but only for a moment.

'Patrick, don't say anything.' A long finger reached out to touch the firm line of his mouth.

He captured it with his hand, pressing a kiss against the tip, then staring deep into her hazel-gold eyes. 'I haven't said a thing for over a year.' Although his statement was quietly stated, the words were drawn through tightly clenched teeth. 'But then I don't have to say anything, do I? We're adults. We don't have to play games, do we?'

'You mustn't say anything,' she replied,

moving an inch or two away. She could see the argument to dispute her statement forming in the set of his jaw, no doubt intending to remind her that her marriage was only words on a piece of paper. 'Please, it won't do any good.'

'Have dinner with me next week.' His request was almost a plea as his gaze roved possessively over her face. 'I'll meet you anywhere you say.'

'It's . . . it's not possible,' she asserted weakly with a confused, negative shake of her head. Desperately she wanted him to sweep away her arguments with sure, masculine ardour, to be a knight slaying all the dragons.

A fragile stillness danced briefly between them. 'Have I been wrong?' Patrick asked grimly. 'Aren't you attracted to me?'

The song ended, the last dying note of the piano ringing mournfully in Tanya's ears as she slipped out of his unresisting arms. She knew she should have sought the company of the other guests, but foolishly she didn't want the hopeless conversation to end.

'What woman wouldn't be attracted to you?' The lightness was forced and brittle. 'You're strong and handsome and unmarried — that's a potent combination difficult for any woman to resist. I find you very attractive, Patrick,' she said quietly, 'which is why I won't meet you outside the walls of this house.'

'What kind of a hold does Lassiter have on you?' he demanded harshly. 'Why are you so afraid of a man you've seen only seven days out of seven years?'

They were standing in the small shadowed corner of the patio, among and yet apart from the other guests.

'Jake has no hold over me.' The cool mask stole over her face, the darkness increasing the marble quality of her complexion. Not even to Patrick, a man she was half in love with already, could Tanya confide the true reason for her loveless marriage. 'My life is of my own making.'

'And none of my business,' he added, snapping a gold lighter to light his cigarette. 'Not even if I want to make it mine?'

For so long, Tanya had stood figuratively alone without anyone but herself to lean on. And Patrick was so strong, so very strong. She pressed her lips tightly together to keep words of surrender from tumbling out.

His quiet persuasive voice came from near her shoulder, the distance between them lessened. 'John needs a father, Tanya,' striking at the vulnerable chink in her armour, 'not someone who exists for him only in name as Jake does.'

'You're not playing fair,' she accused in a voice that was shaking with anguish and self-doubt.

'All is fair, Tanya.'

'Excuse me, I have to go check on John.' She hurried away from him, suddenly afraid she would give in to the temptation dangling so tantalizing in front of her.

As she approached the sliding glass doors,

Julia Lassiter intercepted her. 'We need some more ice at the bar. Would you bring it out, Tanya?'

'I'll get it,' Patrick spoke up, a step or two behind the women. Tanya glanced at him quickly, surprised to find he had followed her. 'Tanya wants to check on John.'

'Thank you, Patrick,' the older woman smiled. 'And give Johnny a goodnight kiss for me.'

'I will, Julia,' Tanya promised, hoping her inner agitation wasn't showing.

Only one light cast a dim glow in the foyer and it was at the opposite end near the entrance door. Tanya turned to face Patrick as he closed the sliding glass door behind them.

'There are bags of ice in the freezer,' she told him quickly.

When she would have turned away, his hand reached out and stopped her, drawing her instead into a corner of the room to take her in his arms. Her lips moved to protest, but Patrick silenced them with a gentle, probing kiss that left her breathless and unable to speak. There was sweet ecstasy in the contented sigh that sprang from his lips when he disentangled them from hers, cradling her face in his hands so he could gaze into her dazed eyes.

'Jake must be insane to leave you behind,' he murmured.

'Yes, I must be.'

With a horrified gasp, Tanya tore herself out of Patrick's arms to stare in the direction from which the voice had come, its insolent arrogance immediately recognizable. Still she stared in disbelief at the man leaning so negligently in the living room archway, yet in total command of the situation.

'You've been gone too long. She isn't yours any longer, Lassiter,' said Patrick in a voice that was deceptively soft.

There was no answering comment. Tanya watched with an unnamed fear paralysing her throat as Jake slowly straightened into an upright position, noticing for the first time the cigarette held in his hand. He moved out of the shadows of the arch to snuff it out in an ashtray, looking taller and broader than Tanya remembered.

He stopped where the light fully illuminated his aristocratic features. The dark tan of his skin made his blue eyes take on the colour of cold steel. 'Come here, Tanya,' he ordered.

His compelling gaze held hers as she unconsciously closed the distance between them, too stunned by his sudden appearance to do anything else. Only two feet separated them when she stopped, her eyes examining his face, noting the changes that had been made in the four years since she had last seen him.

His face was leaner and more uncompromising than before. The softness of youth had been stamped out by the hard experiences of life, the lines in his face now exhibiting a harshness and unrelenting strength. Jake was still handsome, but now with more rugged overtones. The virile masculinity was the dominant factor in his attraction, that along with a world-weary cynicism.

His study of Tanya was just as thorough. 'You can go now, Raines,' he directed with mocking sarcasm, his gaze never leaving Tanya's tilted head.

The sound of the glass door sliding shut released Tanya from the shock that had held her silent. Disdain glittered coldly in her eyes. 'Nothing has changed,' she stated, allowing her lip to curl with sarcasm.

'You damn little bitch,' he muttered savagely, reaching out to grasp her shoulders, his fingers digging through the fragile material of her dress. 'I expect more of a welcome from my wife than that!'

He pulled her against his body until every muscular inch was pressed against her, evading, then capturing the fingers that would have clawed at his eyes, and twisted her arms behind her back. Brutally he covered her mouth that had moments before trembled under the sweetness of Patrick's kiss. Her lips were ground against her teeth, the taste of blood in both their mouths. The iron band of his arms was crushing her into senselessness, bringing a reeling sensation to her tightly closed eyes. Tanya had no breath to struggle, however uselessly, as Jake continued taking his sadistic pleasure with her lips.

Then he let her go, derisive amusement in his eyes that he had conquered her so easily. 'What's the matter?' he mocked, openly laughing at the burning fires of hate in her face as Tanya fought for the breath that had been denied her. 'Wasn't it as *genteel* as his?'

'You pig!' she spat, striking out with her hand at the sarcastic expression on his face and thoroughly enjoying the biting sting as her palm made contact with the hollow of his cheek.

With the swiftness of a striking cobra, he captured the guilty hand, turning her fingers into a painful ball of flesh, while his other hand grabbed a mass of her hair and twisted her stiff body against his.

'I knew that sophistication was a pose,' he sneered. 'You're the same untamed hellcat I brought into this house seven years ago.'

'Let me go!' she hissed, her eyes burning from the pain inflicted by his cruel tugging of her hair that forced her to look into his face.

'Let her go, son.' J. D. Lassiter's quiet voice came from the patio doors.

One corner of Jake's mouth curled contemptuously at the limp relief that caused Tanya to sag weakly against him, rescued at last, or so she thought, from her husband.

'In a minute, Dad,' he answered arrogantly. 'I want to make sure my wife knows how good it is to be home.' Mockery underlined every word.

His hold on her slackened. Her eyelids fluttered down as Tanya realized gratefully that she would soon be free from his inhuman treatment. Then, through the thickness of her lashes, she caught a glimpse of tobacco brown hair, the only warning she received before her lips were taken again. His mouth was sensually masterful. Tanya didn't respond nor resist, jolted by the fire born inside her from the spark of his touch. The contact was brief, ending before she had recovered sufficiently to struggle free.

Anger flared immediately in her amber eyes, drawing a throaty, mocking chuckle from Jake. His finger lightly touched the tip of her nose.

'That's the way to welcome a man home, honey,' he grinned, turning away from her before she could retaliate, to walk to his father. 'It's good to be back, Dad.'

Tanya watched the warm reunion between father and son, her body trembling with the violence of her emotions while her hands were clenched in useless fists at her side.

'I can't begin to say how glad I am to see you, Jake,' J.D. declared fervently, their hands still clasped together in greeting. 'You've come back none too soon.'

'That thought has been driven home to me several times these last two days,' Jake agreed cryptically, sliding a blue glance at the volatile expression on Tanya's face. 'And never more sharply than tonight.'

Her usually attractive mouth was set in a grim line, refusing to rise to his baiting reference to the scene he had witnessed between her and Patrick. That last kiss had made it evident that he hadn't been living a celibate existence these last

40

years, and his subtle criticism only put her temper on a shorter fuse.

'Mother will be so happy to see you,' the older man shook his head, chasing the last remnants of disbelief away as he continued to gaze into Jake's face, drinking his fill like a thirsty man. 'Damn this party!' J.D.'s voice was choked with emotion. 'I have a half a notion to send everyone home.'

'And I thought you'd killed the fatted calf to welcome me back,' Jake smiled.

'I would have if I'd known,' his father returned gruffly. 'Did you know, Tanya?' he asked, finally releasing Jake's hand and turning towards the rigidly still girl. 'Was this some present for our anniversary?'

For all the outward air of rejoicing in her father-in-law's expression, Tanya saw the searching look he gave her, assuring himself that she was unharmed. Some of her anger faded as she remembered the firm reprimand J.D. had given when he had ordered his son to let her go.

The smile she gave him was tremulous but sincere in its warmth. 'It was as much of a surprise to me as it was to you.'

'That's true, Dad.' Jake's eyes seemed to rest on her face with lazy indulgence, but Tanya saw the metallic hardness gleaming through and returned it with a glittering challenge. 'Tanya was possibly even more surprised than you.'

Tanya wished in fuming silence that there was a way to end his double-edged comments without lowering herself to reply in kind. Sensing the electricity crackling invisibly in the air between them, J.D. walked over and put an affectionate arm around her shoulders.

'Your wife is an absolute gem,' he declared. 'And that boy of yours — he keeps your mother and me both young.' The glass doors to the patio slid open, averting the three pairs of eyes to the woman entering the house, and interrupting any caustic comment Jake might have made.

'Hello, Mother,' Jake said quietly.

Julia Lassiter brushed a hand in front of her eyes before letting it fall to the blue brocade bodice of her dress. 'Jake?' Her voice broke, as she took a hesitant step towards him.

'I'm home. Happy anniversary.' Then he was folding his arms around the happy, sobbing woman. Tanya's blood ran cold as she glimpsed the tender, charming smile given to her mother-in-law, recalling too vividly the effect it had once had on her. 'No more tears, Mother,' Jake teased, lifting her quivering chin with his hand. 'I don't want them spoiling the face of the most beautiful mother in the world.'

'I'm so happy,' Julia declared, smiling through the receding tears. 'When did you get back? Did you know he was coming, J.D.?'

'I had no idea, Mother.'

'I didn't let anyone know,' Jake explained, planting a lingering kiss on his mother's tear-stained cheek, 'in case something happened that I couldn't come.'

'How long will you stay?' Her glance bounced

42

off Tanya, who guessed Julia was really wondering if she was going to drive Jake away again.

'I don't know for sure.' A hint of harshness laced his voice.

'Oh, Jake, please, you must —'

'Now, now, Mother,' J.D. placed a restraining hand on his wife's shoulder, 'we'll save those discussions for another time. Let's just be grateful he was able to come home.'

The trio of Lassiters seemed to huddle together, drawing a circle that put Tanya outside its circumference. She had always known she didn't belong, that her presence was suffered only because of John. That was the way she wanted it, she told herself, asserting her independence with a proud lift of her chin.

With Julia monopolizing the conversation, Tanya slipped quietly from the foyer, walking quietly down the hallway to her bedroom, assuring her pride that she was only leaving to look in on John. But the instant the door closed behind her, she leaned against its firm support. The mirror on the opposite wall reflected the pallor in her face, and she had to admit that Jake's unexpected arrival had taken a considerable toll on her nerves.

A clawing surge of loneliness rose up, threatening to tear out her insides. She closed her eyes against the aching emptiness that assailed her, opening them to see that her reflection had a self-deprecating smile on its face.

Only two weeks ago she had been sitting on a

rock near the top of Dewey Bald Mountain. There, with the spring mating calls all around her, she had acknowledged her own growing longing for a mate, accepted that the never-satisfied restlessness consuming her was the desire for a man's attention.

After seven years of abstaining from any form of caress, she had been kissed three times in one night by two different men. It would have been amusing if it wasn't for the sickening knot in the pit of her stomach. Why was it that her lips remembered so vividly the provocative caress from Jake and so vaguely the sweetness of Patrick's? Shame and self-disgust ate away at her. The desires of her flesh had made her so weak as to ignore the dictates of her mind and become aroused by the sensual kiss from a man she loathed. Tanya had always believed she exercised complete control over her senses. She had for seven years.

Of course, there had been mitigating circumstances. She had only moments before suffered the humiliating punishment of Jake's first embrace, if it could be called that. The shock of his return, the intimate scene he had witnessed, and his cold-blooded assault had all combined to wear down her defensive barrier. Rationally she could see how her guard had slipped when freedom from his touch seemed imminent.

Now that Tanya realized how susceptible she really was to, evidently, any man's caress, she convinced herself that she was better able to cope with it. Jake Lassiter was a dangerous man, more so now than he had ever been because there seemed to be a ruthless determination about him. His actions quite plainly said that he would take what he wanted, his years in some of the primitive regions of Africa stripping away the veneer of civilization.

In those last few moments during which she had an opportunity to mull over the sudden turn of events, a degree of composure was restored to Tanya. The quaking anger had receded, allowing her hand to pick up the hairbrush from the dressing-table without trembling. A few quick strokes through her streaked tawny hair put its long length back to its usual state of order, although her scalp still tingled at the back where Jake had so roughly tugged at it.

The bathroom off her bedroom had a connecting door into John's room. Tanya used it, quietly entering the room to spy the boy sound asleep, the light still on beside the bed, but the television was off. An unquenchable love brought a warm smile to her lips as she tiptoed over to draw the bedcovers around the pyjama-clad figure. She lingered for several minutes before brushing a light kiss on the smooth forehead and whispering 'good night'. She flicked the lamp off as she left the room.

One step inside her own room Tanya froze, staring at the long, lean form stretched out on her bed. An overhead light fully illuminated the room and the lazy, mocking expression on the face Jake turned towards her, his head resting comfortably on his hands. The rich blue of her satin quilted bedspread emphasized the white of his shirt opened at the throat, tapering from the wide shoulders to the dark brown trousers over the slim hips. Potent, masculine virility struck out at her with the force of a body blow.

'Aren't you going to order me off your bed?' he taunted softly.

Tanya bit back the angry words that would have done just that. Instead, she chose to take a calmer attitude. 'Why should I?' she shrugged indifferently, walking over to the mirror to flip the ends of her hair needlessly with a comb.

'You didn't expect me to come back, did you?' Jake lithely swung his legs over the edge of the bed to sit on the side, at the same time joining his reflection in the mirror with Tanya's.

'No, I didn't,' she said, coolly meeting the mockery in his eyes.

'I don't know why you didn't. I practically heard a trumpet fanfare when I received your letter,' a sneering, droll sarcasm in his voice.

'You make it sound as though you never heard from me,' Tanya snapped. 'I wrote you a letter every week, which is more than could be said for you.'

'A letter? Is that what you called those impersonal pieces of paper I received?' Jake laughed in his throat, the chill of his blue gaze contemptuously holding hers. ' "I took John to the dentist today. John enjoyed his first day of

46

school. John is learning to swim." Never once was there a "How are you" or "What have you been doing", just short and bitter-sweet messages to fulfil your duty. What was I supposed to write back? The bulldozer broke down today? I stopped off and had a beer with the boys last night?'

'Perhaps if you had, John wouldn't have got this ridiculous notion that he didn't have a father!' Her temper flared in spite of her determination to keep it under control.

'You would have liked that, wouldn't you? It would have suited you just fine if I never returned,' he jeered. 'How it must have grated to write that last letter to me reminding me of my duties as a father!'

Tanya didn't trust herself to speak. The venom on the tip of her tongue would only make an intolerable situation worse. The yellow flame in her eyes watched Jake uncoil and walk over to tower behind her.

'If I wanted to shirk my responsibility as a father, I would never have married you!' His vicious statement stripped away the colour in her cheeks. 'Or did you forget that in your attempt to keep me as black as your memory paints me?'

Their eyes clashed in the smooth glass of the mirror. 'I never suggested that you take that post in Africa,' Tanya answered calmly. 'Nor did I ever tell you to stay.'

'Why did you marry me, Tanya?' His eyes narrowed into thin slits of ice-blue contempt. 'From the first there was nothing but loathing in your eyes when you looked at me, and a silent wish for my early demise. You never gave our marriage an opportunity to work. Why should I have stayed? John was a baby. He needed his mother, but not me. And you made it clear every time you looked at me how much you despised me.'

'I never asked you to marry me,' she reminded him acidly, 'only to acknowledge John as your son.'

'The instant you had my money you would have run away to the remotest place, taking my son with you so I could never see him again.' His perception brought a quick rush of colour to her cheeks. 'The reason I married you is the same reason that I'll never divorce you. I want my son, even if it means putting up with you.'

It was Tanya's turn to emit a sarcastic laugh. 'Your son is seven years old. He doesn't even know what his father looks like, nor is he even sure he has one. How do you reconcile that with this great paternal love you profess to have?'

The sudden tightening of his jaw told her that her arrows had found the target. Then one corner of his mouth curled upwards. 'Seven years we've been married,' Jake said dryly. 'To quote an old joke, it seems like only yesterday, and you know what a lousy day yesterday was. Time has a way of slipping past. I admit I didn't intend to stay away so long, but John is only now reaching the age when he needs both parents, as you pointed out in your letter. You've come of age too, Tanya.' His hands spread around her waist, their scorching touch turning her to face him. 'Those curves I felt against me tonight belonged to a fully grown female.'

She stared down at his arms, slowly raising her eyes to his face so he could see her distaste of his touch even while her heart thumped wildly against her ribs. 'There's no point to this discussion,' she declared in a frost-tipped voice. 'It's time I was returning to the party.'

His hold tightened fractionally when she started to move away. 'Has Patrick Raines become your lover?' The metallic hardness of his gaze belied his drawling voice.

'No!' The explosive denial came too quickly, accompanied by an uncomfortable rush of warmth to her face. 'Tonight was the first time —' she bit back the rest of the words, suddenly angry that Jake had drawn any kind of an explanation from her.

A wide, triumphant smile split his face, his eyes gleaming with amusement as he released her waist. 'Then I did come home in time!'

'You came back because of John,' she asserted sharply.

'I'm not about to forget the reason I'm here,' he agreed smoothly. He picked up the jacket he had tossed on a chair, slipped it on, and turned with a mocking bow towards Tanya. 'Shall we join the party?'

CHAPTER THREE

Julia caught sight of them before anyone else as Jake and Tanya walked through the sliding glass doors. She hurried over to them, her hand reaching out for her son's arm while her gaze rushed lovingly to his face.

'Did you look in on Johnny?'

'Actually John was asleep,' Tanya began, only to have Jake lightly touch her arm to stop her.

'I looked in when I first arrived,' he said, sliding a mocking glance at Tanya's surprised expression. 'He'd fallen asleep before the bugler sounded the charge that brought the cavalry to the rescue in the movie he was watching.'

'Isn't he a beautiful child?' Julia declared, ignoring Tanya's sudden silence. 'He looks just like Jamie when he was a boy. There's no mistaking that little Johnny is a Lassiter.'

'None at all,' Jake agreed. There was no amusement in the expression he turned to Tanya. 'He looks like a fine boy.'

Was he praising her? she wondered, finding the ensuing rush of pleasure at the thought to be quite unsettling. But at that moment, Jake's presence was noticed by some of the other guests and Tanya's attention was distracted from that disturbing discovery.

All the other men wore suits and ties, which made Jake stand out all the more with his informal open-necked shirt. Yet Tanya was forced to acknowledge that even in evening attire he would be conspicuous. There was an aura of power and self-possession about him that rejected the restrictions of convention.

His hand rested on the curve of her hip, keeping her at his side as he renewed old acquaintances and made new ones. It was a gentle and unnecessary reminder that she was his wife and one that she resented while parrying the comments of the guests on Jake's unexpected arrival.

Mrs. Osgood had just declared, 'You must be terribly happy to have your husband home after all this time,' when Tanya spied Patrick walking towards them with his sister.

'Not half as happy as John will be,' she qualified, forcing her gaze away from the rigid line of Patrick's face to the woman standing in front of her.

'That's your little boy, isn't it? Does he know his daddy is home?'

'He was sleeping when Jake arrived.'

Tanya started to edge away from the light hold, not wanting Patrick to see the possessive touch, but her movement was stopped by Sheila's airy voice. She managed a passing nod in the direction of the departing Mrs. Osgood while turning to stare at the brunette bestowing a more than

51

affectionate kiss on Jake's cheek.

'You're full of surprises, Jake,' Sheila scolded provocatively. 'You could have mentioned that you were going to be flying home. I would have kept your little secret.'

'I hadn't made my decision then,' Jake replied, amused and even pleased at the intimate look the dark-haired girl was giving him. 'And I hadn't realized how many reasons I had to come back.'

To Tanya's knowledge, Jake and Sheila had never met. Sheila would have only been fifteen when Jake had married Tanya and it was inconceivable that he had met her on his only other trip home four years ago.

Sheila cast a sideways glance at Tanya, her dark eyes amused by the confusion written in her expression. 'Didn't Patrick tell you?' Sheila asked with mock innocence. 'I went along with him on his overseas junket a month ago. That's when I met Jake.'

Tanya darted a quick glance at Jake's unrevealing profile before looking to Patrick for confirmation, noting the hint of exasperation around his brown eyes. 'I thought it was a company trip,' addressing her half statement, half question to Patrick.

'It was,' he asserted.

'I persuaded him to take his little sister along for a little vacation,' Sheila spared an overly affectionate glance at her brother. 'Of course, he was so busy flying back and forth between Europe and Africa that I finally stopped trying to keep up with him and stayed in Africa. I would have been bored to tears if Jake hadn't been able to take a few days off.'

A slow boil was seething through Tanya at the implication behind Sheila's words. 'No, Patrick didn't mention that.' The undertone in her voice added that her husband hadn't either, which placed a smug smile on Sheila's artfully bowed lips. 'How fortunate for you that Jake was able to get free.'

'I imagine Sheila would have been able to keep herself amused if I hadn't been there,' Jake smiled lazily, his eyes roaming familiarly over the girl's face. 'But, since I did have some slack time, I thought it was only right to keep an eye on the sister of the firm's acting manager.'

'Is that what you were doing?' Sheila murmured seductively. 'Keeping an eye on me?'

Jake must have felt Tanya breathe in deeply to control her temper at the sly innuendoes Sheila was making because there was a fractional tightening of his fingers on her waist. She arched him a speaking look. He couldn't possibly think she cared one way or another whether he had had an affair with Patrick's sister. She merely found the thinly veiled insinuations disgusting.

'I'm glad you found my husband's company so diverting,' Tanya declared with cloying sweetness. 'It would have been terrible if you'd been marooned in a strange country with no one to show you the sights.'

'We didn't do much sightseeing.' Sheila

53

flashed a coy look at Jake before returning her demure countenance to Tanya. 'Although I did want to tour the construction project Jake was working on. But he explained to me that some of the crew hadn't seen a woman in weeks and there was no reason for them to be needlessly aroused when the job was so near completion and they would all be returning home to their wives and families soon. I'm glad Jake didn't think it was necessary to impose those restrictions on himself. Of course, he didn't decide to return home until after I left. Did I act as a catalyst for your decision?'

'Let's say you reminded me of some of the compensations there would be to returning home.'

White-hot anger seared through Tanya at Jake's complacent drawling voice. She was denied the privilege of freeing herself from his suffocating hold on her waist by his own movement to light a cigarette. The haughty expression in her tawny eyes taunted him with the knowledge that his supposed concern for his son wasn't the only thing that had brought Jake back. It was obvious Sheila had been a contributing factor. Behind the gauzy cloud of exhaled smoke, his arrogant features mocked her indignant air.

'How long will you be staying, Jake?' Patrick inquired with the same deceptive softness he had used earlier.

'Are you asking me as an interested bystander or as an executive of the firm?' There was a knife-edged challenge in the look Jake threw at him.

'A bit of both.'

There was the barest tightening of Patrick's square jaw as the two men silently took each other's measure. Then Jake let his gaze slide over to Tanya, curving the sensuous line of his mouth into a smile that didn't approach the hardness in his eyes.

'Danvers has more than enough experience to handle the road project, so you need have no fears, Raines, that I left an untidy mess behind me.' He took a long drag on his cigarette, then studied the fiery tip through narrowed eyes. 'There's every probability that I'll be staying here a very long time.'

Each word of his statement was slowly and carefully enunciated so there could be no mistake about what he was saying.

Tanya stared at him helplessly, trying to fathom the unreadable expression in his face as Jake displayed interest in his cigarette while the impact of his announcement made its mark. Not an hour ago he had told his mother he didn't know how long he would be staying. Had Sheila's presence influenced his decision? It seemed obvious, and yet was it? Tanya had no doubt that Sheila was a factor, but not the deciding one. It was clear that Jake didn't intend to enlighten them as to the cause.

'I believe that calls for a drink,' Tanya announced, finding herself in need of a medicinal dosage of alcohol to restore her shaken composure. 'Excuse me.'

'I'll help you,' offered Patrick, moving quickly to her side.

'Make mine something festive and bubbly,' Sheila ordered gaily. Her words only confirmed what Tanya already knew — that she found Jake's announcement something to be celebrated.

Patrick stepped behind the portable bar to mix the drinks as if sensing that her hands weren't steady enough for the task. She gripped the padded edge of the bar fiercely, turning her knuckles white in the process.

'Why didn't you mention that Sheila went with you on your trip?' lowering her voice so that her question was for Patrick's ears alone.

'She is my sister, in spite of the gap in our ages. It was a case of Sheila wanting to take a trip as I was leaving on one.' His dark gaze raised to dwell thoughtfully on Tanya's face. 'Or are you really asking why I didn't mention that she had become — acquainted, shall we say, with Jake?' The slightly piercing quality made it difficult for Tanya to meet his look squarely. 'Frankly,' he continued when it became obvious that she wasn't going to reply, 'I had the impression that you didn't care what your husband did as long as he stayed away. I'm beginning to think I need to revise that opinion.'

'He means nothing to me!' she denied quickly. 'I just felt so idiotic standing there with everybody knowing what was going on but me.'

'Tonight — when I all but told him to get lost — why did you go to him when he called? Why did you leave me standing there like a fool while you rushed to his side?' Patrick demanded.

'It was shock.' Tanya ran a nervous hand over her tawny hair. 'A nightmare. I couldn't believe he was really there. I never thought he would come back. Not even when I wrote —'

The muttered expletive from Patrick stopped the tumbling torrent of words. 'You asked him to come back?' he ground out harshly.

'I had to.' Her eyes begged for his understanding. 'Not for myself — for John. He had this crazy notion that Jake was dead or in prison, and insisted on writing a letter asking his father to come home. What else could I do?' she ended with a resigned shake of her head. 'You'd mentioned how busy Jake was. I hoped . . . I thought he wouldn't be able to get away.'

'Yes, I remember,' Patrick sighed, running a hand wearily through his dark hair. 'It's just when I think about you being alone with him later on tonight, I —'

Searing hot fires leapt through her at Patrick's implication and Tanya hurried to banish the image of her in Jake's arms. 'His bedroom is across the hall. We don't —'

'Haven't you got those drinks mixed yet, Raines?' Jake's voice slashed out at them from his position just behind Tanya. She spun around to stare into the cold anger on his face.

'My, but you two look guilty,' Sheila declared with kittenish delight. 'What were you whispering about?'

'Scotch and water all right with you, Jake?'
Patrick asked, deliberately ignoring his sister's
jibe as he handed her a drink.

'Scotch and water is fine.' Tanya met his
chilling gaze defiantly, refusing to feel the tiniest
pinprick of guilt over her completely innocent
conversation with Patrick.

'What shall we drink to?' Sheila demanded,
darting a coquettish look at Jake over her up-
raised glass. 'To your homecoming?'

'Let's make it something we can all drink to,'
he suggested dryly. 'Shall we say — to better days
and brighter tomorrows.'

Their glasses made a semblance of touching
before they were raised to their lips. The bracing
swallow of liquor had little effect on Tanya, not
with the way Jake kept watching her, that and the
sullen silence from Patrick.

They were still standing near the bar, so there
was always someone stopping to have a word
with Jake and eliminating the opportunity for
any more double-edged exchanges. Tanya
moved to the side, appearing to be a part of the
quartet but holding herself aloof while deliberately avoiding any eye contact with her husband
and wishing she had never written the letter that
had precipitated his return.

'Well, Jake,' a man exclaimed with a good-
natured slap on his shoulder. 'What are you
going to do with yourself now that you're back?'

'The first thing I'm going to do is spend some
time with my family,' he announced. Sliding a

58

glance at the darting look Tanya gave him before breaking contact quickly, 'and get acquainted with my son.'

'It's too bad he's in school right now,' Sheila murmured. 'You're going to have a lot of empty hours during the day.'

'I'll think of ways to fill them.' A twisted smile lifted the corners of his mouth as Jake stared into the veiled promise in her dark eyes.

The man missed the interchange between Jake and Sheila as he laughed, 'I imagine the little woman will have a lot of plans that will only include the two of you. Isn't that right, Mrs. Lassiter?'

The colour washed out of Tanya's face as she met the arrogant and amused smile on Jake's satirical features.

'Jake makes the plans,' she smiled, not caring that she sounded like a dutiful wife bowing to the wishes of her husband. He would know that what she really meant was his plans didn't include her.

'If only my wife were that amenable!' The man widened his eyes expressively.

'I never thought of Tanya as being amenable,' Jake declared with a mocking glint in his eyes.

'Jake, the Harrises are leaving,' his mother touched a hand to his arm. 'Come and say goodbye to them.'

'Of course.' He nodded his excuse to the gathering as he wound his way through the thinning guests towards the sliding doors.

'Come on, Sheila. It's time we left, too,' said

Patrick, reaching out to take his sister's arm. His dark head inclined towards Tanya. 'I'll see you?' he murmured.

A cold hand closed over her heart, making her feel unnaturally chilled. Her troubled eyes met his questing gaze. 'Yes, Patrick,' she nodded absently, acquiescing because her thoughts were too tangled to make any coherent protest. Sheila flicked her an amused glance as she bade her an airy goodbye.

Their departure seemed to signal an end to the party and a general exodus of the remaining guests began. As she repeated the polite words of parting, Tanya kept glancing towards the doors, expecting Jake to return before the last of the guests left. But there was no sign of him when the final couple departed and she breathed a sigh of relief.

There was still a sound of voices in the foyer and in the front of the house, indicating her mother and father-in-law were occupied, probably along with Jake. Tanya didn't want to chance a meeting with him inside, so she busied herself with collecting the glasses and scattered dishes on the patio, placing them on a trolley to be later wheeled into the house.

Not a breeze stirred the air. The silence of the night was broken only by the distant, eerie cry of a screech-owl. Tanya paused near the far edge of the patio, turning her face up to the midnight sky with its smattering of stars and shimmering pale moon, savouring the stillness of the moment before a dim red glow caught her eyes among the trees. As she turned towards it, she saw a dark form separate itself from the shadows to make its way to the steps, artfully constructed to appear like natural stone formations. Tanya stiffened when the moonlight glistened on the bronzed tan of Jake's face.

'I thought you were saying goodbye to the guests,' she accused.

'I slipped away when nobody was looking.' He didn't glance her way as he reached the empty patio and sank into one of the cushioned chairs, taking a last drag on his cigarette before crushing it out in an ashtray. He was still carrying his drink and held it in both hands to stare with a frown into its pale amber depths.

'Why?' Tanya demanded, feeling an uncontrollable urge to bait him the way he had done all night. 'Were you trying to figure out ways to meet Sheila on the sly? It shouldn't be too difficult. She usually spends the summers on Patrick's houseboat tied up at one of the marinas. It should prove to be a convenient rendezvous spot for you!'

Two shafts of cold steel bored into her until he blocked her out of his vision by swallowing the remaining liquid in his glass. 'Actually I was tired,' Jake said with thinly disguised impatience. 'I've crossed quite a few time zones since I left Africa.'

There were lines of tiredness increasing the harshness of his face, but Tanya could summon no sympathy for him. Instead she directed her attention to the empty glass in his hands.

'Are you through with that, or do you want another drink?'

A bitter grimace chased across his mouth. 'One is my limit now.'

'Really?' she deliberately made her voice sarcastic as he rose to his feet to place the glass on the trolley in front of her. 'That doesn't sound like the Jake Lassiter I remember.'

'No, it probably doesn't. I recall a night when I got so drunk that I couldn't remember a thing, and less than a year later a girl shoves a baby under my nose and tells me it's my son. An experience like that has a very sobering effect on a man.'

Her gaze fell under the austerity of his. Her stomach twisted itself into knots as she tried to appear as calm as Jake, but her hands were trembling visibly. Tanya clasped them together, vividly aware of the way he towered over her and the muscles that rippled under his jacket.

'I've often wondered,' Jake continued when his statement was only met with silence, 'what you recall about that night.'

Tanya stared at her hands for a minute more before defiantly tossing back her head to meet his bland gaze. 'The mind is a compassionate organ. It blocks out the unpleasant memories.'

He didn't appear the least disconcerted by her biting voice, lazily meeting the contempt in her blue eyes. 'Was everything about the evening unpleasant?' he asked without giving her time to reply. 'The whole night wasn't completely blacked out for me by drink. The first part is relatively clear. I remember meeting a very lovely and shy young girl at the Sedalia fair and asking her to dance with me. I even remember how prettily she blushed when I told her that her hair reminded me of skeins of antique gold. We didn't talk very much, though. I just held her in my arms and made a pretence of moving my feet so it would seem as if we were dancing while I stared into those topaz eyes.'

His voice was like velvet, weaving a magic spell that turned back the clock to that night. Tanya had only to shut her eyes to have that deliciously heady sensation take possession of her at the thrill of being in his arms. She remembered that first tender kiss and the second that had been filled with such fierce passion. That was when she had fled from him, frightened by her own response and the desire that flamed inside her. A steel door clanged in her mind, shutting out the rest of her memories of that evening.

'What are you trying to make me believe?' she demanded bitterly. 'That you actually cared about me? That I meant something to you? Was I really any more to you than a one-night stand?'

His hands captured her shoulders, giving her a hard shake. 'Tanya, damn it! I —'

'You were going to come and see me the following weekend — or so you said!' she accused shrilly. 'You never meant to, and we both know it.'

'My brother was killed in a car crash. I couldn't come,' he ground out savagely.

'That was convenient, wasn't it?'

There was an exasperated movement of his brown head at the sarcasm in her voice and he dropped his hands from her shoulders, running a hand through his hair. 'I don't even remember telling you I'd come back. But I intended to until Jamie was killed.' The weariness in his voice was not caused only by lack of sleep. 'To be perfectly honest, nothing seemed to matter very much after he died. I'd almost forgot you existed until I accidentally ran into you.'

'That I can believe,' Tanya agreed bitterly.

'That's why you hate me, isn't it?' He held her gaze, refusing to let her look away. 'Your ego was hurt because I took you and forgot you. You couldn't even forgive me for that when I married you. You felt I owed it to you to marry you, to partially pay for one imprudent night.'

'That's not true,' she protested, stung by the heartless picture he had painted of her. 'I never intended you to know about John, not until we met accidentally . . . I never wanted to marry you, but when you found out about John, you threatened to take him away from me. The only reason I told you about him was —' the muscles in her slender throat constricted and she had to wait a moment before continuing. 'I told you because I wanted you to squirm, to feel some of the guilt and shame that I had. I only wanted money to take care of the bills. But you wanted the baby!

You and your Lassiter money and Lassiter power and Lassiter name! First I'm treated like some cheap little tramp and forgotten, and then I'm supposed to be forgiving when you make me marry you in order to keep John! You ask the impossible.'

His mouth was drawn into a grim, forbidding line. 'You've never tried. We have never treated our marriage as any more than a masquerade. For our son's sake, it's about time we did. You admitted that much when you wrote that letter suggesting I come back, even if you didn't think I would come.'

'It won't work, Jake.' He seemed too close to her and Tanya took a quick step backwards, some unreadable light in his eyes sending her senses reeling.

'I never said it would work!' he exclaimed with a flash of angry impatience. 'I said we should try. No marriage will work if the two people involved won't try. You're a beautiful and desirable woman, and I can't believe you find me totally repulsive.'

If only she did, Tanya wished silently, looking anywhere but at the compelling male face. 'What are you asking, Jake?' She spoke quietly, the hidden fear showing in her eyes when she glanced at him. 'That I go to bed with you?'

A cynical noise that resembled laughter sounded in his throat. 'I know you probably think I've been in the tropics so long that my blood always runs hot,' he jeered. 'The answer is no, I'm not asking you to go to bed with me, although it might be the ultimate answer. What I do want you to do — or suggest that we do — is to treat each other like friends instead of enemies. To try to get to know one another as we really are and not any preconceived notion as to what we think each other is like. Call it a trial period or a truce or whatever, but we need to bury the past.'

'It's an excellent theory,' Tanya agreed, gazing out into the tree-shadowed darkness of the night so he couldn't see the slight wistfulness in her eyes. 'I might even have considered it if it weren't for the contemptible way you treated me tonight.'

'You mean when I caught you kissing Raines?' Jake asked, lighting another cigarette with studied nonchalance.

'He has a first name. It's Patrick!'

Her quick defence only drew an amused smile. 'I probably do owe you an apology for the way I manhandled you. We may be man and wife in name only, but I still consider you to be mine. I suppose seeing you in his arms was a blow to my male pride, and your insolent coolness didn't help.'

Tanya was quick to note that Jake never actually apologized, only admitting that he should, but it did mollify her a bit.

'Well? Will you consider a trial period?' Jake repeated, watching her through half-closed eyes.

'What about Sheila?' she asked stubbornly, part of her knowing she didn't dare agree to his offer.

'She doesn't enter the picture at all.'

'Doesn't she?' She arched an eyebrow in his direction. 'You seemed quite glad to see her to-night. And you must have got to know each other rather well when you were in Africa together.'

He seemed to hesitate before replying. 'As for Sheila, there are times when a man needs a woman, disgusting as it must sound to you, and that's the only explanation you're going to get.' His admission of an intimacy with Sheila didn't bring the least glimmer of remorse or discomfort to his expression. 'But our agreement would be strictly between the two of us.'

'Are you saying that you won't see Sheila?'

'Are you saying that you won't see Patrick?' Jake countered swiftly, his eyes narrowing on the rosy hue of her cheeks.

'I told you I haven't been seeing him!' Her temper flared at his implication that she was as unprincipled as he.

'After tonight, I don't think he's going to be satisfied merely to gaze at you from afar. The taste of honey is addictive,' a sardonic smile touched his mouth. 'But that's beside the point. You still haven't answered whether you'll agree to my proposal for a truce.'

'What happens at the end of this trial period if I still despise you?' Tanya demanded.

'If, at the end of two or three months, we don't feel our marriage could be in any way successful, then we'll have to explore the alternatives,' Jake told her.

'Divorce?' Tanya wondered why the word seemed to stick in her throat.

'That would be the obvious one.' Not even the layered clouds of cigarette smoke could hide the piercing regard of his eyes.

'And if I don't agree to your so-called truce, what then?'

'Then things will continue on exactly as they are.' There was no mistaking the inflexibility in his words.

'That isn't much of a choice, is it?' Her amber eyes smouldered with her outrage.

'It depends on the way you look at it,' he said smoothly. 'Think it over and give me your answer in a couple of days.' The next instant Tanya was staring at his retreating back.

CHAPTER FOUR

Tanya rolled over on her back, pressing a hand against the dull ache in her head. Golden ribbons of sunlight streamed from her bedroom window. She sighed wearily without knowing exactly why. An odd depression seemed to be casting shadows over the morning and only when she blinked her eyes open did she remember the cause.

Jake was home.

With a little moan she buried her head in the pillow, her memory racing back over the events of the previous evening. He was back with the intention of staying. No longer would she be able to ignore the existence of her husband. The worst of it was, she couldn't summon any hatred for him, only a nameless fear of the repercussions his return could bring and the terrifying thought that living with her day in and day out might enable him to guess the secret she had guarded so carefully.

The door to her room burst open and John came tearing in. He catapulted himself to the side of the bed, stopping there to catch his breath as Tanya pushed herself into a sitting position.

'Is it really true? Is my dad really here? Grandma said he'd come home. Where is he?' The rapid-fire questions were hurled at her with unrestrained eagerness.

John was too excited to notice that Tanya's smile was forced. 'Yes, he is here. He's in the other bedroom sleeping.'

'I'm going to go and see him!'

Before Tanya could reach out to stop him, he had whirled around and headed for the door. 'John, wait!' she called sharply, swinging her feet on to the floor and reaching for the layered white chiffon robe to cover the silk of her nightgown.

By the time she could cover the same distance to her bedroom door, John was flinging open the door on the opposite side of the hall. He stood poised inside the door, one hand still holding the knob when Tanya reached him.

'Don't wake him, John,' she whispered firmly, her fingers settling on his shoulders to draw him silently out of the room.

Then her peripheral vision saw the reason for John's transfixed stance. Jake was standing in the doorway to the private bath. Dark blue trousers moulded his thighs and hips, but his chest was bare and very tanned. His thick, tobacco-brown hair still glistened from a shower while the clean scent of soap permeated the air. Amused blue eyes took in Tanya's dishevelled appearance as an uncomfortable feeling of warmth stole over her face. Then his virile gaze swung down to the boy standing in front of her.

'Good morning, John. You are John, aren't you?' Jake asked with a decided twinkle in his eyes.

The silken brown head nodded affirmatively as John continued to stare at the man whose presence dominated the room. 'Are you my dad?' his small voice asked, a hint of doubt in his words that indicated that he was bracing himself for a denial.

Jake's answer was a simple and unequivocal, 'Yes.' But he made no move towards the boy.

Tanya discovered she was holding her breath. Very quietly she expelled it as she gently removed her hands from John's shoulders. The room was so still a feather could have been heard landing on the carpet. Finally John released the door knob and walked slowly towards Jake, stopping when he was directly in front of him to tilt his head back and look up at Jake.

'Will I be as tall as you are when I grow up?' he asked seriously.

Jake smiled, a slow smile that transformed his carved features into an expression of unbelievable tenderness. He kneeled down to be at eye level with the boy.

'You might even be taller,' he answered just as seriously.

There was another period of silence, but without the tension of the first. Tanya watched the pair knowing they had completely forgotten she was there in the room. They were so close together, yet not speaking or touching. One was

71

standing, his gaze questing and exploring the face of the stranger who was his father, and the other kneeling with a confident and understanding expression. 'Have you had breakfast yet?' Jake finally asked.

'No.'

'Neither have I. Why don't you run and ask your grandmother to put another plate on the table and we'll eat together?'

John nodded a quick agreement and turned to leave, then stopped and turned back to the still kneeling man. An adult-like frown creased his forehead.

'I'm glad you came home Dad,' he announced firmly, then spun around and dashed from the room.

Jake slowly straightened to his feet. Eyes as calm as a summer sky met her tawny gaze.

'I'm sorry,' Tanya murmured helplessly, clutching her robe tighter about her throat.

'Why?'

'John's welcome wasn't exactly enthusiastic. I —' She stared down at the carpet. 'I'm afraid he doesn't know you very well.'

'Did you expect him to throw himself in my arms? I would have been disappointed if he had.' He met her startled glance blandly. 'I'm a stranger to him. I wouldn't want him to give me his trust and affection simply because he's been told that I'm his father. It's a much more precious gift if it's earned.'

Tanya sighed. 'I suppose you're right.' Her

fingers raked through her tousled hair. She couldn't shake the feeling that she was ultimately to blame for the cleft between father and son. She didn't hear the catlike steps that brought Jake nearer to her.

'Give him time to get to know me, Tanya.'

Her pulse raced in agitation as she realized how close he was to her.

'Have you thought any more about our discussion last night? A friendly truce would be the best thing for John.'

From the corner of her eye, Tanya could see the even movement of his bare chest calmly breathing in and out. Part of her mind couldn't concentrate on what he was saying because of the potency of his animal attraction.

Her voice was a hoarse whisper when she did reply. 'We can never be friends, Jake.' She dredged up the strength to look warily into his face and saw the tightening of his jaw at her adamant stand.

'I never said we could be friends,' he corrected sharply. 'In fact, I would be the first to admit that it's practically an impossibility. All I want to do is get rid of this damned hostile atmosphere that we're both guilty of fostering.'

'I don't know. I just don't know,' Tanya asserted with a shake of her head, her eyes looking everywhere except at the man standing beside her. His semi-nakedness was evoking a primitive response on her senses, making her too vulnerable to his harsh persuasion.

73

She expected storm clouds to descend at her indecisive answer. She wasn't prepared for the sudden softening of his tone, like the caress of velvet over her skin.

'Is a peaceful co-existence so much to ask?' His hands reached out to grasp the upper portion of her arms.

The thinness of her chiffon robe couldn't ward off the scorching fire of his touch, nor could her senses fight the desire to be drawn against the muscular strength of his chest. Tanya closed her eyes tightly and cringed to elude his hold, her hands raising upwards to protect herself from any further advances.

'Don't touch me!' she gasped, her voice trembling violently at the traitorous response of her body. 'I can't stand it!'

Her eyelids fluttered open to see the fists clenched rigidly at his side while the polar temperature of his gaze froze the expression of pain in her eyes.

'How did I ever marry a frigid little piece of baggage like you?' Jake sneered with a mixture of contempt and self-contempt. His eyes mercilessly raked her from head to bare toe. 'You have the wrappings of a beautifully passionate woman, but there's nothing inside except ice!'

'No!' Her pride protested, unable to let his scathing words stand without a denial, knowing full well her problem was she was too susceptible to a man's attention. 'That's not true!'

His face took on a cold, seductive quality that

chilled even as it attracted. 'I'm from Missouri. You're going to have to show me.' His softly spoken jeer carried an unmistakable invitation to come in to his arms to prove her claim.

Her breath caught in her throat even as Tanya swayed closer to him, drawn by an irresistible magnetic force. His glittering gaze held her captive, pulling her nearer when every instinct cried for her to flee. As his warm breath fanned her cheeks, her glance flitted to the sensual line of his lips. Her own ached to feel his possess hers, to inflame the desires she had kept banked for so long. At the last second, Tanya knew she couldn't let Jake discover her dangerous vulnerability to a man's caress.

He must have sensed the beginnings of her withdrawal and reached out to fold her in his arms, the blue fire in his eyes dwelling on the parting softness of her mouth. 'Don't chicken out now, honey,' he chided softly.

There was a rush of footsteps in the hall before John came to a halt in the open doorway, his eyes opened wide at the seemingly embracing couple. He blinked twice before stammering out his message.

'Grandmother says . . . your breakfast i . . . i . . . is ready.'

Jake smiled down at Tanya's lowered head, silently and humourlessly laughing at her rigid arms that were uselessly trying to push him away. 'Don't worry,' he whispered scornfully in her ear, 'you've been saved.' As he relaxed the steel band of his arms that had held her, he directed his son, 'I'll be right there.'

John shifted uncomfortably from one foot to the other, unsure whether he was supposed to stay or go. Tanya's feet were rooted to the floor as an embarrassing wave of shame and humiliation washed over her. But Jake was very calmly putting on a shirt, buttoning it and tucking it into the waistband of his trousers, not the least bit shaken as Tanya was over what almost occurred. Before he left the room with his son, he walked over to her and raised her chin to gaze into her tear-blurred eyes with complacent satisfaction.

'You did try, Tanya. Maybe next time,' he murmured.

'There won't be a next time,' she retorted.

He merely raised an eyebrow, a mocking gesture that indicated more plainly than words his disbelief, then he released her and turned away.

'Are you ready, John?' his bland voice asked.

'Are you coming, Mom?'

'No.' Tanya quickly swallowed the rising sob of panic, adding more calmly, 'I have to get dressed yet. You go ahead with your father.'

She brushed a hand over her cheek, wiping away a tear that had fallen from her damp lashes. A small hand touched her arm.

'Are you all right, Mom?'

'Yes, I'm fine.' But the weak smile she gave him wasn't reassuring.

'Why are you crying?' John darted an accusing

look at Jake standing in watchful silence at the door, his features deliberately unrevealing.

One word. That was all it would take, and Tanya knew John would turn against his father. One spiteful word and she could destroy the tenuous thread of their relationship. For a moment there was a glitter of vengeance in the gold-flecks of her eyes. How simple it would be to pay Jake back for every wrong she believed he had done. She glanced towards Jake, seeing the hardness in the blue depths of his eyes that knew the power she had over his son's love.

'I'm crying —' Tanya took a deep breath and looked down into the thin, apprehensive face, 'I'm crying because I'm happy, John. Because your father has finally come home.'

There was a hint of uncertainty in his face before it was wiped away with a large smile. His perception was still that of a child's and he couldn't see the defeat dulling her eyes.

'So am I, Mom,' he agreed.

'Your breakfast is getting cold,' she reminded him. The hand that touched his cheek affectionately was trembling. 'Run along before your grandmother sends out a search party.'

'Come on, Dad,' John called, waving to Jake to follow him as he hurried past.

But Jake was looking at Tanya. Her sense of fair play had brought her figuratively to her knees, but it hadn't bowed her head. He studied her for a minute more before he turned to catch up with the small boy. Tanya wondered if Jake realized she had just declared him the victor before the battle had begun. But not all the spoils of war would be his. At all costs she must ensure against that.

The days following Jake's return fell into a pattern. The daylight hours when John was in school Jake spent with his father, going into the company office in Springfield or staying at their lake-front home. Late afternoons and early evenings were devoted to John. Sometimes they went fishing or played ball or, if spring rains forced them inside, they watched television together or played draughts.

The late evening hours, the ones Tanya dreaded most, had been entirely in the company of his parents. Only for odd moments were they alone and Jake had allowed her to keep the conversation on a safe topic. But she had the feeling that he was only biding his time, waiting for his own moment to force an agreement out of her. She shuddered to think what the consequences might be if she should consent to a trial period for them to get to know one another. Tanya wanted to spend no more time alone with him than she had to in order to maintain an outward appearance of peace to his parents. And her pride wouldn't let her bolt every time he stepped into a room where she was.

Today — Saturday — Jake had taken John boating. Tanya had been able to exclude herself from the excursion because of a previous commitment to help with a sale of work held by the women's organization of their church. Each woman had volunteered for a three-hour shift and hers was about over. She scanned the small crowd for a glimpse of her mother-in-law who should be arriving to take her home.

Instead Tanya saw a tall, dark-haired man weaving his way towards her. With a start of guilt she realized she hadn't given Patrick Raines a single thought since that first night when Jake returned. Looking at the dark curling hair with its silver wings at the temple and the strong, handsome face, she felt the familiar feeling of warmth encompass her as it did every time she saw him.

'Patrick, what are you doing here?' Her cheerful smile was completely natural and not the least bit forced.

'I was out at the house with your father-in-law. Julia was getting ready to leave just as I was, so I volunteered to come in her place,' he explained. 'Are you ready to leave?'

Tanya said her goodbyes to her replacement at the cake-laden counter and walked with Patrick to his car. He flashed her a warm smile as he opened the door for her, then walked around to the driver's side.

'I've missed you,' Patrick said simply as he slipped the car into gear and reversed out of the parking lot.

'It seems much longer than last week since I saw you,' Tanya answered truthfully, tilting her head back to feel the refreshing breeze blowing in from the car window.

'I wasn't sure I would be welcomed if I came. I know Jake wouldn't be glad to see me,' he laughed without amusement. 'And I couldn't help wondering if his return had changed your thinking as well.'

He tossed her a questing look that Tanya was oddly reluctant to meet. It was funny how before last week when the silence had been broken and the first tentative words had been spoken, she had imagined them meeting like this, stealing a few minutes alone. Now she found herself uncomfortable and unwilling to bite into the forbidden fruit.

'You know you're always welcome as far as I'm concerned,' she managed to answer with an air of unconcern that ignored the deeper meaning of his question.

'Why did he have to come back?' Patrick muttered, his strong fingers closing over the wheel in a death grip. 'You're already withdrawing from me. I recognize the coolness in your voice. I've heard it too many times at parties when someone has got overly friendly and you wanted to put them in their place. I thought you felt something for me.'

With a stab of guilt she knew she had let him believe she did. In truth, she was drawn to him, but too afraid of the consequences.

'I do . . . that is, I could,' she corrected quickly. Her words threatened to tumble over themselves in a rush to get out. She determinedly breathed in deeply to gain control. 'I have more than just myself to think about, Patrick.'

'You mean John. Well, you can't honestly say that Jake has been much of a father to the boy,' he grumbled.

'That's as much my fault as it is Jake's.'

'I find that hard to believe,' he sighed. 'Do you believe in love at first sight?'

'No!' The violence of her answer surprised her until she remembered how completely she had been taken in by Jake's charm so many years ago, before he had so unutterably destroyed her illusions about life and love. 'No, I don't,' she repeated more calmly.

'In a way, I believe in it.' His dark eyes roamed over her perfect features. 'I was still married the first few times I remember seeing you. Even then I found you attractive. I kept growing more curious about you, about why you and the Lassiters maintained this air of a perfect marriage between you and Jake, and yet you still never visited him and he never came to see you. I found myself growing jealous that you might have a lover on the side. I couldn't figure out why until I realized that I wanted to be that man. That's when I began to see that shimmer of loneliness in your eyes. You are lonely, aren't you, Tanya? That self-possession is just a front, isn't it?'

'Everyone is a little bit lonely,' was as much as she could admit before tilting her head back proudly to show it didn't matter.

'You don't have any family, do you? I want to

know everything about you,' Patrick asserted with grim determination. 'Were you an orphan?'

'Not really. My parents were killed when I was nineteen. I was already out on my own by then supporting myself,' she answered calmly.

'No brothers or sisters?'

'I had a younger sister,' Tanya stared out the window. 'She died of pneumonia a few months after we lost our parents.'

'You were about nineteen when you married Jake, weren't you?' But Patrick didn't look to her for confirmation. 'That must have been a rough time for you. I can see how you could have wept on the first shoulder offered. That's a blow anyone would have trouble handling. What happened, darling? Did you fall in love with love and only realize when it was too late that it was a mistake?'

The sympathy in his voice cried out to her. She very nearly unleashed the whole story to him with every sordid detail, but somehow she held back.

'Yes, it was something like that,' she agreed.

'Sometimes it's a mistake to try to hold a marriage together for the sake of a child, which is what you're trying to do. Have you ever asked Jake for a divorce?'

'We've discussed the possibility.'

'I'm —' Patrick began.

'Please, let's change the subject,' Tanya interrupted, the beginnings of a headache pounding in her temples.

'I'll be glad to drop the subject,' sighed Patrick, giving her a look that was passionate and grimly stubborn, 'if you'll tell me where I stand.'

They had already turned off the main highway on to the road leading to the Lassiter home. Patrick slowed the car down and parked on a layby in the road overlooking Table Rock Lake.

'Well, Tanya?' he repeated.

'I don't know.' She pushed her long tawny hair behind her ears and stared at the mirror-like body of water reflecting the surrounding hills in the afternoon sun. White clouds danced gracefully in the blue sky. 'I haven't had time to think.'

'I'm a man, Tanya. Now that I've touched you, I can't be content to gaze at you from afar.'

He was close beside her when he made the last statement, his hand on her shoulder slowly turning her towards him. His words were so nearly the same as the ones Jake had said that Tanya wanted to laugh hysterically. Only when she looked into Patrick's eyes, it wasn't so funny.

Without a protest she allowed him to draw her against his chest, hoping in the contradictory turmoil of her emotions to find solace there. But her uncertainty only seemed to be intensified. The lips that touched her hair and moved down to brush her eyelashes produced a warm sensation, yet not nearly as soul-destroying as Jake's caress.

'I'm not the kind of man to beg,' he murmured against her cheek. 'But I want you, Tanya.'

She moaned a protesting 'no' as his mouth

moved to cover hers and his arms tightened when she tried to pull away. All emotion drained away as she lay passively in his embrace, knowing that subtly she had invited this advance and finding she didn't really want it. Yet her lack of response didn't discourage Patrick. There was still an ardent fire in his dark brown, nearly black eyes when he released her and shifted back to his own side of the car.

'Now do you understand the way I feel about you?' he asked, his breathing ragged and uneven. 'I don't want a hole-and-corner affair any more than you do. I understand how you feel about your son and I respect you for it. You want him to have a good home, a decent education, and a future. The Lassiters can give him all of that and the security of a family. You just say the word and I'll give him the same things. Young John likes me. I think he would accept me as his father. He's certainly seen more of me than he ever has of Jake.'

Tanya stared at him in bewildered amazement, not believing that he was actually proposing to her. 'Are you asking me to leave Jake and marry you?' she breathed.

'That is exactly what I'm asking.' He smiled at her tenderly, his strong features made all the more handsome by the love shining in his eyes. 'I even have the urge to get down on one knee and repeat it.'

'But I'm not even sure that I love you,' she protested weakly, looking away before she succumbed to his persuasive charm.

'I'd be the last one to ask you to change one husband for another that you don't love either,' Patrick nodded, wisely not pushing her on a decision. A wistful smile played over his mouth. 'You have no idea, Tanya, how badly I want to court you and win your love. I want to see you again, alone, like this, where we can talk and not be afraid what we say will be overheard, even if it's only for a half an hour or an hour — whatever you can arrange. Say you will, darling?'

'I don't know when I —'

The sound of another car's tyres on the gravel halted her hesitant agreement. She saw the quick frown that appeared on Patrick's forehead even as she turned her head to see the approaching car. Her stomach fell with sickening suddenness as she recognized Sheila sitting beside Jake at the same moment that they saw her with Patrick. Jake said something to Sheila that drew an expression of displeasure as the car halted beside them. The grim look on his face when he stepped out of the car did little to ease the frightened hammering of Tanya's heart.

'You don't have to explain anything,' Patrick said quietly, a reassuring hand closing over hers. 'We've done nothing wrong.'

She cast him a grateful glance as her door was opened and Jake leaned down to mockingly look at the occupants. Tanya braced herself for the tirade that was to come.

'Admiring the view?' Jake inquired calmly, his

steel blue eyes glancing towards the expanse of lake water below them. 'It's a lovely spot this time of year.'

'Very beautiful,' Patrick agreed, the challenging gleam back in his eyes.

'Sheila got tired of waiting for you to come back, so I volunteered to take her home. It's a good thing I ran into you. It saves both of us making the trip.' His hard blue gaze turned on Tanya. 'You can ride back to the house with me.'

Patrick's expression was plainly saying she didn't have to go with Jake if she didn't want to, but Tanya smiled to let him know she didn't mind.

'Thanks for picking me up,' she told him.

Before Tanya had a chance to retract her decision, Jake's hand closed over her arm, propelling her out of Patrick's car to his own. Sheila's mouth was turned petulantly down at the corners as she crawled reluctantly out of the car to make room for Tanya.

'I so looked forward to you taking me home, Jake,' she sighed meaningfully, 'but I know you're anxious to get back to your little boy. I'm glad you asked me along today. I did have a marvellous time. Maybe we can do it again?'

The last was accompanied by a bewitching smile directed solely at Jake, who returned it with a half-promising, 'Maybe.' Tanya found her anger rising as Sheila blew him a kiss and hopped gaily into the car with her brother. Patrick's car was nearly out of sight by the time Jake walked leisurely around his own and slipped behind the wheel.

'Did she go with you and John today?' Tanya demanded, her eyes flashing a glance at the man calmly lighting a cigarette before starting the car. His casual attire of pale tan slacks and a brilliant blue knit shirt suited his muscular physique and the bronzed features below his slightly wind-ruffled brown hair.

'As a matter of fact, she did, although it wasn't planned that way,' Jake replied with a derisive smile.

'Poor John must have put a terrible crimp in your style,' she retorted sarcastically. 'What a pity you promised to take him along.'

'It was Sheila who wasn't part of the plan. John and I bumped into her when we stopped at the marina for lunch.' His gaze explored her face. 'The time we spent together was as innocent as your few minutes with Raines.'

Tanya turned away from his searching eyes, knowing the warmth in her cheeks had betrayed her sense of guilt.

'Of course,' Jake continued, a chilling coolness invading his tone, 'you didn't have the benefit of John as a chaperon, so perhaps yours wasn't quite as innocent.'

The censorious accusation in his voice angered her. He didn't actually believe that she was as lacking in morals as he.

'Our meeting was motivated by more respectable reasons than yours,' she retorted.

'Respectable?' he jeered. 'Would you like to explain that?'

She shifted uncomfortably in the leather-covered seat. 'Patrick asked me to marry him.' Her voice was coolly composed.

A darting glance took in the way Jake's head was arrogantly thrown back, but the anger that was briefly shown in his eyes quickly vanished as he studied his cigarette.

'I have to give the man credit. I didn't think he would move as fast as this,' he said, surprising Tanya with the indifference in his voice. 'What was your answer?'

'That's my business.' She stared down at her hands, trying to figure out why she felt so disappointed by Jake's calm acceptance of her announcement.

'It's mine, too, Mrs. Lassiter.' He underlined the last with mocking emphasis. 'If not as your husband then as the father of our child.'

'If you must know, I didn't give him an answer!' Her anger returned as quickly as it had fled.

'Why?'

'Because I didn't have a chance. Your unexpected arrival didn't show the best of timing,' she retorted sarcastically.

'If you'd had the chance, what would it have been?' Jake persisted.

With a belligerent toss of her head, Tanya turned to stare at him, the false words of her acceptance of the proposal forming on her lips. But she found she couldn't be less than truthful under his penetrating regard.

'I don't know. I need time to think it over,' she said, keeping the defiant lift to her chin.

'It doesn't sound to me as if you're really in love with the man or you wouldn't need time to think.' His comment was accompanied by a twisting smile. 'You certainly can't plead that you don't know him. You've known Raines as long as you've known me.'

'But I don't know you,' she protested artlessly.

'Do you want to?' Jake asked softly with a glitter in his eyes that attacked her breathing.

Tanya sat motionless, afraid she would say something else that she would regret as much as her previous admission. Very slowly she gained control over her clamouring nerves and shook her tawny hair in a negative movement.

'No, I don't,' she said firmly. 'What I do know about you, I don't like. There would be no point in expending energy on a useless cause.'

'Are you saying our marriage is a useless cause?' There was speculation in his narrowed gaze.

'What would you call it when we can't even be in the same room together without the air being filled with a sort of seething tension?' she countered nervously.

'Is that the way you feel?' But he didn't seem at all upset by her description and merely shrugged when she nodded her assertion. He turned the key in the ignition. 'Maybe you're right.'

CHAPTER FIVE

Tanya slipped out the patio door into the warmth of the moonlit night. She had just tucked John into bed and the idea of returning to the living room where Jake and his parents were was too oppressive. A solitary walk along the lake's edge was much more inviting. She was determined to let none of her problems intrude on the beauty of the evening.

Streamers of stars adorned the heavens while the moonshine cast silvery shadows on the rocks and boulders along the path that she walked. Crickets and cicadas sang out their shrill songs, drowned out now and again by the distant scream of a screech-owl, or the baying of a hound. A breeze tickled the tops of the trees, an assorted collection of oaks, cedars and hickories, but it didn't penetrate the foliage to fan her cheeks.

It was a languid night, warm and humid and still. A lopsided three-quarter moon gave the Lake's mirror surface a pearly sheen. Tanya paused near the private pier leading out to the boat dock, then turned to wander out over the water, her footsteps on the planks sounding unnaturally loud. She stopped at the end and leaned over the railing to stare into the hidden depths.

Her skin felt hot and sticky where her clothes persisted in clinging and the water looked so deliciously cool. There were no other homes or resorts on their little cove and no running lights from boats were visible. Tanya was completely alone. She removed the leather clasp that held her tawny hair back, swept it on top of her head and secured it again. The small locker on the dock always had a towel inside which she quickly removed and laid near the railing. Before she could have second thoughts, she stripped off her clothes, placed them near the towel, then used the ladder to slip into the water.

After the first shiver had passed from the cold water touching her bare skin, a sensuous kind of enjoyment took over. Treading water for only a few seconds, she struck out for open water with the rhythmic strokes of an experienced swimmer. For over a quarter of an hour she alternately swam and floated in the moon-kissed water. When the initial spurt of energy passed, the cold water began to make itself felt. She turned with a leisurely sidestroke to head towards the dock.

Perhaps it was a sixth sense or the betraying glow of a burning cigarette or the creaking of a wooden plank caused by human weight that made her aware that she wasn't alone. She stopped several yards short of the ladder, her eyes searching the shadowy areas near the boat-house for her intruder.

'Who's there?' she called out sharply.

There was a movement as a tall figure dissoci-ated itself from a dark corner and walked to the railing directly in front of her.

'I didn't know mermaids could talk.'

Even before the softly spoken words were car-ried across the water to her, Tanya had known the voice would belong to Jake. She very nearly reversed her course and struck out for the oppo-site shore, but she knew she was too cold and tired to make it.

'Please go away, Jake.' The chattering of her teeth made the order sound more like a plea.

The moonlight played over his wide forehead and prominent cheekbones, throwing the hol-lows of his cheeks in sharp relief while accenting the white gleam of his teeth as his mouth opened in an amused smile.

'It's not a mermaid,' he teased with a mocking, regretful sigh, 'only Mrs. Lassiter skinnydipping in the moonlight. That water must be cold.'

'It is!' she snapped, trembling with cold and anger. 'Will you go away so I can get out?' But Jake continued to lean against the rail staring at her. Tanya was infinitely grateful for the ebony depths that hid her nakedness, fighting the em-barrassing sensation that his gaze was piercing the darkness. 'If you won't go away, then toss me the towel from the ladder.' She hated the des-perate ring in her voice, but her limbs were beginning to feel numb and she didn't know how much longer she could continue to tread water.

Jake glanced where she had indicated, took a step, then leaned down and picked up the towel. He held it in his hands and looked back at her, laughter etched in every carved line of his face.

'If I throw you this, you won't have anything to dry off with,' he reminded her tauntingly.

'I'll worry about that later,' she retorted, hating him for catching her in such a humiliating predicament.

With a shrug, he tossed it in the water ahead of her, forcing her to swim closer before the towel became soaked and sank beneath the surface. It was impossible to remain afloat and wrap the towel around her in the open water. She had to move to the ladder where she could slip a leg through the lower rung, thus keeping herself upright while leaving her hands free to manoeuvre the towel. Her eyes tossed daggers at Jake, who continued to stare arrogantly down his straight nose at her. She longed to order him to turn his back to her, but knew such an edict would be met with open mockery. Instead she twisted around so her back was to him, fighting the sopping towel until she managed to pull it tightly around her chest and tuck in the end flap. Even secured, the heavy weight of the water-sodden cloth threatened to pull it off as she struggled up the ladder.

'Such modesty!' Jake chuckled. 'I've seen naked women before.'

Tanya tossed him a venomous look as she stalked waterily past him. 'But not me!' she snapped.

'That's a strange thing for the mother of my son to say.' The softness of his voice didn't hide the curious speculation her statement had aroused.

For a split second Tanya froze, a white-hot rush of heat enveloping her shivering body. She managed to put the right degree of contemptuous disdain in her voice. 'An intemperate seduction scene doesn't always require the removal of one's clothes.'

'Damn you!' The expletive phrase was muttered almost exasperatedly beneath his breath. In one fluid stride, Jake was at her side, his fingers bruising her shoulders where they dug into her skin. Tanya was made vividly aware again of his superior height and physical strength, tempered into sinewy muscles by the years spent in Africa. 'Why do you persist in making it sound as if I raped you?'

Her smooth white throat was exposed as she tilted her head up to stare calmly into his angry eyes. 'You can't remember, can you?' she taunted, surprised at her own audacity to provoke him further yet knowing her acid tongue was the only weapon she had.

The burning rage faded from his eyes, replaced by a haunting grimness mixed with pride. His hands fell away as he remained standing rigidly in front of her. 'No. No, I don't remember,'

Jake admitted through gritted teeth. His cold gaze roamed with deliberate slowness over her body half covered by the wet towel that concealed her naked skin while it revealed the mature fullness of her breasts, her slender waist, and the gentle curve of her hips. 'God help me, I can't remember.' He pivoted sharply away from her, a large hand gripping the back of his neck in a rough massage.

Without the intense scrutiny of Jake's eyes, Tanya bent down and picked up her clothes. Her eyes kept straying towards the broad, straight back and the rigid shoulders. Something in the proud, lonely stance closed over her heart with a painful squeeze. She tried to ignore the poignant tug as she walked quietly towards the enclosed boathouse. When she reached the door, she knew she couldn't leave him like that, shouldering all the blame.

'Jake.' Her low voice asked for his attention. The glint of the moonlight shone over his tobacco brown hair as he turned partially towards her in acknowledgement, revealing his aristocratic profile. 'It wasn't rape,' she whispered, slipping inside the boathouse as he turned.

A footstep sounded on the wooden floor of the dock as she quickly closed the door behind her. With apprehensive stillness she waited to see if Jake would pursue her to gain a more explicit statement. There was no further indication of movement following her and she sighed in relief and flicked on the light switch. The wet towel

95

slipped unneeded to the floor as she shook out her olive green slacks. Then a rap on the door had her draw the slacks protectively in front of her.

'There should be a towel you can use on the front seat cushion of the boat, Tanya.' Jake's voice came quietly from the opposite side of the door.

She spied it almost instantly. 'I've found it,' she answered, discarding her slacks to rub the rough textured cloth vigorously over her skin.

Once dressed, Tanya stood hesitantly at the door, overcome by an auspicious feeling that when she opened the door, events would occur beyond her control and ones she might come to regret. There was no alternative. She couldn't stay in the boathouse all night.

Jake was standing at the far end of the dock where a small bench was attached to the railing. One foot was raised on to the seat, his knee acting as a support for his arms to lean on, while the smoke from a half-smoked cigarette curled in a silver gauze cloud around his head. As the door clicked shut behind Tanya, he turned and straightened, grinding the cigarette out beneath his foot. They stared at each other for a long moment before she broke free of his gaze and moved towards the pier leading to the shore.

'Tanya, don't leave yet.' The peremptory ring in his voice halted her.

'Please, Jake, I don't want to talk about that night.' She turned quickly as he came to a stop behind her, her tawny eyes pleading with him not to ask any more questions. Her heart did a somersault at the gentle fire in the depths of his blue eyes.

'I only want you to know that I appreciate your honesty.' There was no mistaking the sincerity behind his words. 'I realize that you didn't have to admit what you did.'

That virile charm was working its old magic on her and Tanya had to look down to break its spell. She couldn't explain to herself why she hadn't been able to let Jake go on thinking as he had. Some inner impulse had compelled her to speak out.

'And I haven't thanked you yet,' Jake continued, 'for remaining impartial about me to our son. So many women in your place would have used him to get back at me.'

'I couldn't do that,' Tanya replied. 'A boy should respect his father.'

'You're a very unique woman. I never realized until now how unique you are. You must have had wonderful parents. I only wish I could have met them.'

But Tanya knew that if her parents had been alive she never would have married Jake. She never would have been driven to the point of mental and physical exhaustion from trying to support and care for a newborn baby alone. Her parents would have been there to share some of the burden. It was quite likely that Jake would never have known he had a son. And those thoughts strangely made her shudder.

'You must be cold,' he declared with a velvet huskiness.

Before she could protest, he had removed the dark gold sports jacket and placed it around her shoulders. Her senses were assaulted by an intoxicating mixture of cigarette smoke, his musky scent of masculinity, and the warmth of his body heat clinging to the jacket. As he moved closer, drawing the jacket together under her chin, the heat emanated from him as if she was standing in front of a blazing fire. Staring at the white polo shirt, she felt the last of her resistance crumbling. When he removed the clasp from her hair, sending it cascading about her shoulders, she knew she wanted nothing more than to be taken in his arms.

He ran his fingers through her hair, smoothing it down around her neck where his hands halted almost encircling her slender throat. Then his thumbs began moving in a slow circular motion that was hypnotically sensuous. The slightest pressure was exerted on her chin, lifting her face towards his. Through half-closed lashes, Tanya glanced up at him, her pulse leaping as she saw his gaze dwelling on her mouth.

'You're beautiful,' he murmured, bringing her closer to him. His breath was like a warm caress. 'I have to do this. Don't fight me, honey.'

There was only submission as he tilted her head back and covered her mouth with his. Submission, until his deepening kiss touched off the passionate core of her soft body spreading a yielding fire through every fibre of her being and Tanya responded. A thousand diamond brilliants glittered in rainbow colours behind her closed eyes. With quaking rapture, she swayed against the solid wall of his chest, her hands creeping up to his neck to twine about it in her own fierce possession.

Yet his hunger for her was insatiable as his hands moved down her back, waist and hips, shaping her feminine form to the hard contours of his body. Tanya strained closer, her heart pounding like thunder in her chest while her mind whirled at the exquisite pain of his crushing embrace. With a driving mastery, Jake parted her lips and began a sensual exploration of her mouth, drawing a moan of sheer ecstasy from deep in her soul.

The jacket fell into a heap on the dock near her feet, no longer needed to provide its impermanent warmth. They were surrounded by a heat wave of their own making, the white-hot fire searing them together. His mouth left a scorching trail over her eyes and ears and neck, then returned to consume her mouth again. Tanya recognized the throbbing weakness in the lower part of her body as the timeless desire for a woman to know a man. The completeness of the intimate longing frightened her and her hands made a fluttering protest against his chest.

His arms tightened fiercely about her, conquering her weak opposition with arrogant sureness. There was a tiny sob of surrender as her lips melted under the ardency of his and her hands began a tremulous and exploring caress of his rugged features. Then his mouth was dragged slowly away from hers and a hand pressed her tawny head against his chest, holding her possessively against him. The rush of his heart was a serenade in tune with the frenzied pace of her own. A wild, sublime peace encircled them for endless minutes, neither wishing to break the mindlessly magic spell.

Then his harsh, uneven breathing became more natural and controlled beneath Tanya's head. His chest rose and fell in one long, shuddering sigh as his hands clasped her arms and reluctantly moved her away from him. Their firm grip prevented her from swaying back to him while she stared at her hands still resting on his waist.

'Look at me, Tanya,' Jake ordered.

Unwillingly she lifted her chin a fraction of an inch, knowing her desire for him was still glazing her eyes. But she obeyed, looking into the smouldering blue flames that burned with the certainty of the power he had over her. His gaze made an intimate exploration of her face, satisfying himself of the response he had aroused.

'Is this the reason for the crackling undercurrents that charge the air between us?' he mused complacently. A smile tugged at the corners of his mouth as even in the moonlight he saw the heightened colour rush into her cheeks. 'Do you still believe our marriage is a worthless cause?'

This moment, more than ever before in her life, Tanya wanted their marriage to be real. Tears sprang to her eyes as the terrible pain of hopelessness struck her abdomen. With a sobbing sigh she lowered her chin, adding a tormented, negative shake of her head.

'It's impossible, Jake.' Her voice quivered with defeat.

She could feel the freezing rigidity flow through him. It was like a knife wound to her heart.

'Impossible?' he echoed angrily. His fingers dug into her arms, giving her a short, vicious shake. 'What do you mean?'

'It can't work.' The constriction in her throat made her voice sound very small and weak. 'There's too much you don't know about me.' She hesitated, afraid of the questions that statement might bring, then rushed on to cover it. 'And I don't know about you.'

'I won't accept that.' There was a return of his haughty arrogance.

'Oh, please please,' Tanya begged, 'can't you leave things the way they were?'

'No,' Jake said grimly. 'It's too late to try to turn back the clock.' The unrelenting hardness of his eyes seemed to pierce through her skin into the hidden secrets of her mind. 'I should have taken you just now and made your submission irrevocable.'

'No!' She took a frightened step backwards,

terrified that he might decide that it still wasn't too late to do it.

'I'm trying to understand you, Tanya, but you're making it awfully hard.' He shook his head in a sort of angry bewilderment and made no attempt to move nearer. 'You said yourself that John needed a father. Well, he needs a mother, too. You can't expect us to spend the rest of our lives sharing a child and still remain strangers to one another.'

'I don't really expect that,' she said with a hopeless shrug.

'What do you expect then? No, no, don't answer that,' he added with a wry shake of his head. 'You'd probably send me back to Africa.'

In spite of herself, Tanya smiled, his droll humour striking a responsive chord. 'Maybe Antarctica this time,' she suggested softly.

His gaze moved to her sharply, a slight twinkle accenting his quiet contemplation of her. 'Today John asked me if you couldn't come along with us some time like Sheila did. Not all the time, but every once in a while.' Jake paused, not really waiting for an answer as he studied her subdued expression. 'We do need time to get to know one another — I said it the first night I came home. That's also why I didn't make love to you the way I wanted to a few minutes ago. If you don't want to spend time alone with me right away, what better chaperon could you ask for than a seven-year-old boy?'

'Oh, Jake, I don't know. I just don't know.' The

admission was wrenched from her heart. She wanted to agree, if for no other reason than to find out if the attraction between them was more than physical. But if it was, what would she gain? She turned away, letting her hands close over the railing.

'Right now we have a son and a marriage certificate. I don't know if we can have a future together or not.' His solemn voice was directly behind her. She made no protest when his hands turned her back around to face him. 'But I do know if we never make the attempt to find out, we'll always wonder if our marriage could have worked. Our chances of making it a success are slim.' His finger gently raised her chin, compelling her to look at the glittering resolution on his face. 'I don't know about you, Tanya, but I'm a true Missourian. I'm going to have to be shown that it's impossible. And I haven't been convinced so far.'

For so many years she had told herself that she hated him. Her mother had often said that it was a very fine line that divided the equally potent emotions of love and hate. Had one been disguising as the other all these years? At the moment that answer eluded her as she stared at the strong mouth and tried to find the courage to answer Jake.

A frown of impatience swept fleetingly across his forehead at her continued silence. 'If you're afraid that I'll take advantage of you, then I'll give you my word right now that I won't touch you.'

'It's not that,' she assured him hastily, finding the thought of being near him and not having him touch her was intolerable. His regard of her took on a lazy, indolent look, almost as though he could divine her thoughts. Tanya swallowed convulsively, trying to appear composed and not at all shaken by the sensuous line of his mouth. 'I don't object to being kissed, although I . . . I . . .'

'We'll go no further than we did tonight.' Jake rescued her from her stammering attempt to qualify her words. 'Unless you specifically ask me to make love to you.'

The amused and knowing glitter in his eyes stole away her poise, leaving her standing defenceless before him.

His arrogant features smiled down at her. 'Are you agreeing to my proposal to get to know one another?'

'Yes,' Tanya sighed, a strange peace settling over her as she made her commitment. Her doubts about the sanity of her decision were momentarily banished.

'This calls for a kiss to seal our bargain, doesn't it?'

Jake gave her time to reply as his head slowly lowered towards hers, but every quaking inch of her wanted to feel that shooting fire his lips were capable of setting aflame. The kiss was short, but without haste, lasting long enough to set her pulse racing before he gently released her mouth. His hands were on her shoulders and she trembled with longing. Jake misinterpreted the movement, deliberately, Tanya thought, as he bent down to retrieve his jacket, placing it back around her shoulders.

'Are you ready to go back to the house?' he asked.

Tanya nodded, knowing that to stay here alone with him would be flirting with temptation. A thrill of gladness swept through her when she turned to retrace her steps and discovered his arm was possessively encircling her shoulders, keeping her beside him as they walked the tight-rope of the narrow pier. Nor did it fall away on the rocky path to the house. She stole one quick glance at his face, noting his pleased, nearly triumphant smile, and wondered if she had made a fool of herself again.

'You won't be sorry,' Jake said quietly, percep-tively reading her thoughts. There was a teasing twinkle in his eyes. 'You might even find I'm a kind of likeable guy.'

Tanya laughed shortly, sending him a rueful glance. 'I think you could charm the stripes off a zebra if you set your mind to it,' she declared.

'In that case,' he grinned, 'a nice little wife shouldn't be too much trouble!'

The way she felt just then she could agree with him, but she wasn't about to admit it. 'The trouble is I don't have any stripes,' she reminded him.

'It isn't stripes I want,' Jake replied as they reached the patio. Tanya was prevented from attempting a comment on that defence-destroying remark by J. D. Lassiter as he moved to let his presence be known. 'Hello, Dad,' Jake greeted him calmly, as though it was the most natural thing in the world for him to have his arm around his wife.

'It's a beautiful night, isn't it?' his father replied after one brief, surprised glance at Tanya. He, too, had a rather pleased smile on his face as he gazed absently at the faint starry ribbon of the Milky Way.

'We took a walk down by the lake,' said Jake, glancing down at Tanya as she shifted uncomfortably away from him. He obligingly let his arm fall to his side, an understanding glint in his eyes.

Tanya didn't feel capable of discussing the trivialities of the weather. She slipped Jake's jacket from her shoulders. 'Excuse me. I feel . . . a little tired. I think I'll turn in.'

There was something very warm and intimate in the look that Jake gave her as he wished her a good night. It went a long way in restoring her shaken composure.

CHAPTER SIX

The first week under their new agreement passed very smoothly, almost as though it didn't exist. Tanya initially thought that Jake might be giving her a chance to back out — which was ridiculous, because Jake wasn't the kind of man to allow anyone to go back on their word.

There had been one short outing, an after-school fishing expedition with John. His delight in having both of his parents along was so pronounced that Tanya felt guilty for not accompanying them before. Not a single 'I-told-you-so' look had come from Jake, only an occasional glance of shared satisfaction at the boy's happiness had been exchanged.

Tanya strolled along the winding private lane, enjoying her leisurely walk to the mail box. Two o'clock. In another three hours Jake would be coming home from his almost daily journey to the firm's office in Springfield, sometimes in the company of his father, but more often alone. It was frightening the way she had begun to look forward to the hour of his arrival.

The shadow of a circling hawk flitted across the ground in front of her as she neared the mail box. She glanced up at the winged predator, admiring the indolent grace of his gliding flight while shivering at the sinister silence of his approach.

'I pity the unwary rodent,' she said aloud as she opened the mail box and riffled through the assortment of envelopes and advertisements.

Her name leaped out at her from the face of one of the envelopes. There was no mistake that it was meant for her and not Julia. It was addressed to Mrs. Tanya Lassiter. Even as she ripped it open, she knew who it would be from. These last few days she had tried several times to compose a letter to Patrick, only to have the words flow stiff and impersonally formal from her pen. With a sinking heart, she read the short message: 'Meet me Wednesday at twelve noon at the Persimmon Tree Restaurant. If you're not there, I will know you couldn't get away. Signed — Patrick.'

Furtively, Tanya stuffed the letter in the pocket of her lemon yellow slacks. She resisted the impulse to dash back to the house and phone him. His secretary was something of a martinet, and it would be impossible to get through her without divulging her name. Since Tanya had never had cause to call Patrick before, her sudden interest in him would set the gossiping tongues wagging.

Tomorrow was Wednesday. She had little time to decide whether she was going to meet him or not. To not go would only postpone things. Patrick would no doubt send another note of a similar nature. She might not be so lucky the next time and someone else might see it first. She had occasionally gone shopping in Springfield, and she would arouse no one's suspicions if she went tomorrow. In that instant, Tanya knew she was going to meet Patrick without confiding in anyone the true purpose of her journey, least of all Jake. Somehow she just didn't believe that he would understand.

Her casual announcement that evening of her plans was taken very matter-of-factly, including Jake. But she didn't escape quite as easily as she had thought she might after Jake spoke up.

'Why don't you meet me for lunch tomorrow?' he suggested.

A quick, apprehensive frown marred her poised expression. What excuse could she possibly give him for refusing his invitation? Her hesitation spoke for itself as did the slight narrowing of his gaze.

'On second thoughts, you'd better not plan on it,' offering her a way out as he leaned back in his chair. 'I might not be able to be free. Lunches invariably seem to turn out to be business meetings these days. Maybe another time?'

'Another time,' Tanya nodded, smiling weakly in relief.

Did he suspect another motive, namely Patrick, for her obvious unwillingness to meet him? She seriously doubted it. Jake was more apt to blame it on a reluctance to be alone with him. Part of her wanted to assure him that that wasn't it at all and explain exactly why she was meeting Patrick, but there was a stronger, cold voice that kept saying it wasn't any of his business.

Dark clouds blotted out the sun. There was an ominous rumble of thunder in the distance increasing the drizzling rain to a steady pour, then allowing it to slack off again. A more melodramatic setting couldn't have been staged for her clandestine rendezvous with Patrick. A hollow humour had dominated Tanya's preparations for the meeting as she had chosen to wear a simple navy blue dress, attractive but not eye-catching. She had sleeked her long hair back into a neat pleat that added severity to her features without taking away their perfection. If the sun had been shining, she thought wryly, she would probably have hidden behind dark glasses.

Still, when she looked at her reflection in the small car mirror, it was hard to believe that the poised, sophisticated woman looking back was herself. No one would guess that beneath that cool exterior she was a trembling mass of confusion and apprehensions. She had never done anything like this before and it made her feel oddly unclean, regardless of how innocent her reasons were. She resolutely thrust aside those feelings of embarrassment and shame that kept bringing unnatural colour to her cheeks. But, as she got out of her car, she glanced unconsciously around to see if anyone was watching. Then she used the umbrella to hide her face as she skipped hurriedly through the puddles of the car-park, not feeling safe until she reached the restaurant doors.

It was twelve o'clock on the dot when she deposited her raincoat and umbrella in the cloakroom. With a deep breath to calm her churning stomach, she walked towards the hostess, her gaze flitting about the room for a glimpse of Patrick.

'How many in your party?' the woman inquired politely.

'Two,' Tanya replied. 'I'm supposed to meet a Mr. Raines here at noon. Would you know if he's arrived?'

'Mr. Raines, yes, of course,' the hostess nodded. 'Come this way, please.'

As she followed the woman leading her down the long, narrow room, Tanya understood why Patrick had picked this particular restaurant. Despite its airy decor of brilliant greens, soft yellows and white, there was also an air of intimate seclusion obtained by the high backs of the white leather booths and the concave wicker chairs that closed around and hid their occupants from view. Patrick's table was in the rear, allowing little chance of their being seen. He rose briefly as she took the seat opposite him.

'I didn't think you would come,' he murmured, an ardent fire darkening his eyes which Tanya couldn't meet.

'I —' she began, only to be halted by a person stopping at their table. She glanced up in alarm.

111

'Would you like a drink, miss?' an attractive waitress inquired.

'No, a cup of coffee, please.' To quiet her jumping nerves, she added to herself.

'We'll order later,' Patrick dismissed the girl sharply, noticing the sudden pallor in Tanya's face followed by an immediate rush of bright pink. He moved to put a reassuring hand over hers, but she hastily drew it into her lap. Neither spoke until after the waitress had returned with their coffee.

'I'm sorry you're so uncomfortable, Tanya. I wish there was some other way we could meet,' Patrick apologized.

'It doesn't matter,' she shrugged nervously. 'I only came to tell you this would be the first and last time I would meet you.'

'What did you say?' A stunned disbelief underlined his words.

'I'm sorry, Patrick. But I just can't see you any more, like this.'

'Why?' he demanded with that incredulous sound still in his voice.

'I tried to write you a letter and explain, but it sounded so cold and trite on paper. That's why I decided to meet you today, so I could explain —' Tanya glanced over at the rigidly set lines of his face, 'that Jake and I have agreed to see if we can't make our marriage work.'

'What?' Patrick's anger exploded around her. He leaned forward, controlling his temper with obvious difficulty. 'You all but told me yourself that your marriage to Lassiter was a farce, perpetrated for the benefit of the boy. Why this sudden concern after seven years of separation to make it a fact?'

'We aren't just suddenly making our marriage a fact,' Tanya corrected stiffly, reacting to his sharp sarcasm. 'It's very unlikely that it will work out at all.'

'If you feel that pessimistic, why did you bother to agree?'

Her motives were too uncertain to bear close scrutiny. If she was falling in love with Jake, as she suspected, there would come a time when she couldn't fool him any longer. Then the little affection and trust she might gain in these next few months would be destroyed. How would she be able to hold him except through John? And could she do that knowing the disgust Jake would feel for her?

Tanya drew a deep, shuddering breath. 'I agreed because Jake indicated that if, after a few months' trial period, we didn't think our marriage could be successful, a divorce would be the obvious alternative.'

Her explanation visibly abated his anger.

'Has divorce never been mentioned before?'

'No, because of John. Since Jake has come home, I believe he's discovered that I've never spoken ill of him in front of John nor attempted to prejudice John against his father. I think Jake feels now that a divorce won't mean the loss of his son's affection and trust.' And that knowledge depressed Tanya. 'The Lassiters have a very strong sense of family ties. Unless I was willing to give up John, Jake would never have divorced me before.'

'Forgive me for being so angry a moment ago,' Patrick smiled apologetically. 'I can understand now why you agreed to go along with Lassiter's proposal. But where does that leave me?'

She had known that question would eventually arise. Some instinct told her it would be futile to ask him to wait — futile for Patrick.

'I mustn't see you any more,' she explained, meeting his gaze evenly so he could see the determination written in her eyes. His strong features took on a bleak look.

'Do you honestly believe Jake is going to stop seeing Sheila?'

Inwardly Tanya reeled from the almost physical blow of his question. She hadn't really known whether Jake was seeing Sheila or not, except for that day she had gone boating with John and him. But Patrick was Sheila's brother and he ought to know.

'I don't know if he is or not,' surprised by the calmness of her response. 'It doesn't affect my decision to not see you again.'

'Is there a reason why I should wait?' He methodically searched her face, a grimness stealing into his expression even before she replied.

'No, I'm not asking you to wait.'

'That says it all, doesn't it?' he announced bitterly.

'I'm sorry, Patrick. I'm truly sorry. I know you're fond of me —'

'Fond of you! My God, that's the understatement of the year!' he muttered, turning abruptly away from the guilty look that appeared in Tanya's eyes. Then in an ominously quiet aside, he asked, 'Did you tell Jake you were coming here?'

'No, of course not!' she replied in a startled voice.

'He's just walked in. No! Don't look around!' he hissed as she started to turn in her seat.

Her stomach lurched with sickening nausea. 'Has he seen us?' she whispered.

'No, I don't think he has. He's with that McCloud man from Denver. They've just sat down at a table and Lassiter has his back to us.' He darted her a cynical glance. 'I take it you don't want him to know that you met me today?'

'No,' she murmured weakly, not able to draw a secure breath, knowing that any moment Jake could walk up to the table and confront them. 'What are we going to do?'

'We can't leave without being seen, so I suggest we have some lunch,' Patrick shrugged, signalling to the waitress that they were ready to order.

Tanya picked at the salad she had ordered and ended up leaving most of it uneaten. Conversation was pointless, considering there was nothing left to be said and it was not a time to be discussing the weather. It seemed as though Jake was lingering an excessively long time over lunch and the minutes went by with nerve-crackling slowness.

'I think they're going to leave,' Patrick announced, darting a quick glance at their table. 'They are. They're walking to the front now. We'll give them a few minutes.'

Tanya felt as if she had been given a reprieve from the death sentence. In all they gave them ten minutes before Patrick escorted her to the cloakroom to get her raincoat and umbrella.

'We should probably leave here separately,' he said.

'Yes,' she nodded in numb agreement. Hesitantly she extended a hand to him. 'I'm sorry the way things worked out, Patrick.'

'Not half as sorry as I am,' he replied, holding her hand for a brief second. 'Good luck, Tanya. I'm afraid you're going to need it.'

Unconsciously Tanya counted to a hundred before she followed the already departed Patrick from the restaurant. The drizzling rain had diminished to a light mist, so she didn't bother opening her umbrella for the short walk to her car. She paused at the narrow drive to allow an approaching car to pass before crossing to the car-park. As it drew closer, she recognized with a growing terror the light blue Seville as her own car, and the man behind the wheel was Jake. Escape was impossible.

The car halted in front of her and Jake stepped out to walk around and open the passenger door.

116

The leashed fury in his expression sent shivers of fear down her spine while the blue polar ice chips in his eyes froze any hope that she could explain. Her legs numbly carried her towards the open door.

'At which hotel are you supposed to be meeting him?' His mouth curled into a derisive sneer.

Pride guided the hand that connected with his face and seconds later kept the tears at bay when he grabbed her by the shoulders and gave her a vicious shake. The cold glints of steel warned her of the rage she had aroused, but the humiliation his accusation had brought wasn't lessened by his anger. Jake shoved her roughly in the car and slammed the door.

Minutes later they were speeding down the highway, Tanya guessing that he was taking her home. She was too miserable to care as he took the scenic back roads at an unlawful pace. His freezing silence was nearly more condemning than his words, and she could have wept with pain. It was an agonizing journey, made more so by the stolen glances in his direction. Every time she gathered the courage to explain why she had met Patrick, it died before the words could ever reach her lips, cut down by the unrelenting set of his jaw.

The instant he stopped the car in front of the garage, Tanya bolted for the house, praying to reach her room before her control collapsed and the tears washed down her cheeks. But Jake was faster, his hand closing over her arm and jerking her back under the overhang.

'Where do you think you're going?' he ground out savagely.

Her words came out with bitter swiftness, uncaring that she was only adding salt to her own wounds. 'To call Patrick, of course, so he won't worry when I don't show up! What else did you think?'

'I'd like to wring your dishonest neck.' His fingers closed over her throat as if he meant to carry out his threat. 'The bargain we made didn't stretch to cover a lover on the side. What did you intend to do? Play both of us along?'

'For your information, I wasn't playing anybody along.' The indignant words had difficulty leaving her tightly gripped throat. 'I met Patrick to tell him I wouldn't see him any more, and I don't care whether you believe me or not!'

The hard, cold expression remained on his face as he stared with uncompromising harshness into her tawny brown eyes shimmering with unshed tears.

'I can't tolerate being lied to,' Jake growled, slackening his hold on her throat. 'If this isn't the truth, I'll find out eventually.'

It was always the 'eventuallys' that frightened Tanya. She closed her eyes, feeling a tear escape her lashes and make a watery trail down her cheek.

'It's the truth, Jake,' she murmured, her eyes blinking open when his hand left her throat. He was staring down his classically straight nose at her face, openly seeking a sign of falseness. 'I thought it was only fair to let him know about our decision to —' Her voice broke in a sob. She bowed her head to fight for composure while brushing the tear from her cheek.

'You crazy, idiotic female,' Jake declared with a humourless laugh. 'When I saw you in that restaurant with Raines and realized that was why you had panicked when I asked you to meet me, I could have cheerfully beaten you both. Rad McCloud had to keep repeating himself because I couldn't concentrate on a thing he was saying. All I could think about was the two of you brazenly meeting in a public restaurant and you thumbing your nose at the agreement we'd just made.'

'It wasn't like that,' she declared. Her voice was choked, but she drew her head back to stare up at him with pride.

His hands reached out, almost touching her shoulders before they fell back to his side. There was an enigmatic quality to his eyes that only told Tanya that the anger was gone.

'I know that now.' He took one of her hands and held it gently in his own. The unconscious circular motion of his thumb had an oddly seductive effect. 'I owe you an apology and this time I do apologize. I should have given you the benefit of the doubt, or at least heard your explanation before I laid into you.'

'You believe me?' Tanya breathed. She hadn't

expected that and it caught her unaware. She wanted to fling herself in his arms and be held there until all the coldness and pain melted away.

'Yes, I believe you.' A ghost of a smile curved his mouth.

'Thank you,' withdrawing her hand and lowering her gaze before she succumbed to her impulse. She moistened her lips, feeling his eyes catch the movement. 'I should have told you what I intended to do.'

'We haven't got to the point of trusting each other yet,' Jake said. 'But look at it this way. This unfortunate incident did allow us to find out more about one another.'

'How do you mean?' Tanya glanced at him warily.

'You've always known I have an ugly temper, but I hope you found out today that I'm capable of admitting I was wrong when I've made a mistake.' His expression was decidedly friendly but nothing more. 'And I've learned that you aren't the type of woman to deceive me deliberately. I'm glad you're honest, Tanya, because I'm not the kind of man who will let himself be used.'

'I think I guessed that,' she swallowed, an unnatural pallor to her skin as she turned away.

'You didn't have a chance to do any shopping,' Jake's low voice followed her. 'Since I have to drive back to Springfield, you're welcome to come along.'

'No. Thank you, but I don't really need anything.' A small, forced smile was sent his direction over her shoulder.

She thought he might follow her, but as she reached the front door, she heard the car door shut and the motor start. Jake was reversing out of the drive as she entered the house.

Tanya was setting the table for the evening meal when Jake returned in the company of his father. The tapping of her mother-in-law's shoes sounded in the hallway as she made her way to the foyer to greet her husband and son. There was a rush of smaller footsteps and Tanya knew John had heard them, too. Setting the last tumbler on the table, she wished that she could casually go meet them too, but she remained in the dining room listening to their voices.

'What have we here, Jake?' she heard Julia ask in a gay voice, followed immediately by John's, 'What's that?'

'It's a present,' Jake replied easily. 'Where's your mother?'

'I don't know,' John answered.

'Setting the table,' Julia replied, a little coolly Tanya thought, her curiosity aroused.

There was a rustle of paper and John saying, 'They're pretty.' Then firm footsteps approached the dining room and Tanya held her breath. Jake was coming to see her. She turned away from the open doorway until the quick glow of pleasure subsided from her eyes. Her fingers moved nervously, needlessly adjusting the silverware beside the china plates as he walked in to stop behind her.

'The table looks fine to me,' he commented lazily, almost as though he knew her readjustment was a pretence to keep from looking at him.

Immediately Tanya began reciting the casual words of greeting. 'Hello, Jake. I heard you and J.D. come in,' beginning to turn to face him. 'Dinner will be ready shortly.'

Her calm expression turned to stunned surprise as she stared at the bouquet of bright orange roses in his hands — a bold, pure orange that was startling in its perfection.

'They're for you. Aren't you going to take them?' There was a gentle amusement in his voice.

Numbly Tanya took the bouquet, a faint rose fragrance tickling her nose. One finger touched the velvet-soft petal of a full bloom to assure herself the tangerine roses were real.

'Do you like them?'

'They're beautiful,' she replied in an awed tone, blinking her rounded eyes in his direction. 'But you didn't have to b—'

'I wanted to do it,' his low-pitched voice replied quietly.

'Because of this afternoon,' Tanya supplied, finding herself saddened that the roses were a gift of atonement for his loss of temper.

'You're not a child to be appeased into good humour by a gift, Tanya,' Jake smiled, the caressing touch of his gaze sent her heart beating a rapid tattoo against her ribs. 'We can't make up for the hurt we've done to each other in the past. We can only try not to hurt each other in the future.'

'Then why the roses?' She stared into the shimmering depths of his eyes, trying to find a motive for his unexpected generosity.

'Simply because I wanted to buy some unusual flowers for an unusual woman. Is that all right?' The tenderly teasing words reached out to enfold her in their warmth.

'Yes,' Tanya breathed, lowering her gold-flecked gaze to examine a rose. 'No one's ever given me flowers before,' she mused, not really realizing she had said it aloud.

'Surely you've received corsages before?' he mocked.

'That's not the same thing,' she denied quickly, glancing into his face to be nearly blinded by the brilliant light in his eyes. Jake redirected his gaze to the rose she had been studying, touching its softness lightly with his hand, while Tanya watched.

'No, I guess it isn't the same thing,' he agreed quietly.

The amused line of his mouth held her mesmerized even as she recognized it coming closer to her. Then his mouth was brushing hers in an infinitely sweet caress that ended much too soon. The swiftly rising colour in her cheeks made it difficult for her to look at him with any degree of composure.

'I'd better put these flowers in water,' she murmured, taking a hasty step backwards and nearly bolting from the room.

Julia was in the kitchen. A curious, almost doubting gleam came into her eyes when Tanya walked in with the roses. She followed her over to the sink as though waiting for some explanation from her daughter-in-law which didn't come.

'They are lovely, aren't they?' Julia finally spoke. 'Why don't you arrange them in the Oriental vase? They would make a beautiful centrepiece for the table.'

'If you don't mind, Julia, I'd rather take them to my room.' Tanya darted a glance at the older woman, loath to share her first gift from Jake with the rest of the family while knowing she was being absurdly sentimental.

Julia Lassiter drew back coldly; her expression was one of just being slapped down after making a friendly gesture. 'Well, of course you may take them to your room. I was only making a suggestion. Jake did give them to you.' Her hurt tone plainly added that she thought she was a more worthy recipient of such a gift.

Tanya sighed, stubbornly refusing to let the hint of rebuke sway her decision to take the flowers to her room as she suspected it was supposed to have done. She knew they weren't red roses, the flower of love. They were only meant as a friendly gesture on Jake's part, but that didn't count as much as the fact that he had given her something that he hadn't felt obligated to do.

'May I still use the Oriental vase?' she asked politely, knowing the exotic orange blooms would look exactly right with the brilliant patterns of greens, golds, blues, oranges in the vase.

'Certainly,' Julia smiled calmly, letting Tanya know that she could be generous and share her things even if Tanya would not.

Later that evening, in the solitude of her room, she singled out the special rose that Jake had touched and pressed it between the pages of her parents' Bible, the only possession she had kept of theirs. She chided herself for giving in to the romantic impulse that had prompted her actions. It was an open admission of love for her husband, a love that she had been fighting because she knew it would eventually bring her unbearable pain.

There was consolation in knowing that love wasn't really love until she had given it to Jake and had it returned. And she was determined that he would never know that she found him more than physically attractive.

Still, it was in the hope of finding Jake that Tanya slipped out on to the patio, trying to fool herself into believing that she only wanted to see him to thank him once again for the roses. But it was his father she found relaxing in one of the cushioned redwood chairs on the moonlight-bathed patio.

'Are you looking for Jake?' he inquired with a twinkle in his eyes, and didn't wait for her reply. 'He's in the study looking over some blueprints and specifications on a new project. I don't think he'd mind the interruption.'

'No, I wasn't looking for him,' Tanya lied quickly, oddly embarrassed by J.D.'s acute perception. 'John is in bed and I thought I'd step out for a breath of fresh air before doing the same.'

'The air is free for the breathing,' he noted blandly, tamping down the tobacco in his pipe before holding a match to it. He gestured towards a nearby chair. 'Sit down. It's a peaceful night.'

Tanya took the chair he had indicated and leaned against the cushioned back, finding he was right; it was a very peaceful night. For long moments they sat in silence; the fragrant scent of pipe smoke was the only thing that reminded her she wasn't alone.

'You and Jake seem to be getting along a great deal better,' J.D. commented quietly through the bite on his pipe.

Instantly alert, she slid a quick glance in his direction to find him studying the bowl of his pipe. But his eyes flicked up to catch her glance.

'You don't hate my son any more, do you, Tanya?'

'No,' she replied without elaborating further. She tried looking the other way, hoping to end the conversation before it had begun.

'When you first came here, I believe every breath you drew was a reminder to hate him for as long as you lived. Of course, time has a way of robbing the satisfaction from making life miserable for a man who made a regrettable mistake.'

'Perhaps that's true,' Tanya sighed. 'Or maybe time puts things in their proper perspective. A person can't condemn a man all his life for one painful hurt.'

'I'm glad you said that.' There was a smile in the older man's voice. 'Maybe there's a chance the two of you can make your marriage work the way it should.'

'I wouldn't count on that, J.D.' Her face was clouded with a wistful sadness. 'That's asking too much of vows taken without love.'

'Love is like a cedar tree. It can grow in the most unlikely places, places where it doesn't seem to stand a chance of surviving. And a love like that, able to surpass all the obstacles, is a most precious thing.'

'Don't — please!' The words were torn from the terrible agony in her throat. 'I know you're trying to assure me that something good can happen after seven years, but don't raise your hopes.' Tears were scorching the back of her eyes. 'A love like that would be a miracle, and I don't think God is giving them away this year.'

'I didn't mean to upset you, child,' J.D. frowned, but Tanya was already rising from her chair to race inside the house. She couldn't let his impossible dream take hold of her heart. Realistically she knew it didn't stand a chance of coming true.

CHAPTER SEVEN

The voices of both small boys were clamouring to be heard at the same time. Jake finally put two fingers in his mouth, emitting a shrill whistle that brought instant silence. Tanya bit back a smile, knowing firsthand how lively two seven-year-olds could be.

'The first place we're going to go is to Grandfather's Mansion,' Jake decreed, holding up his hand as John groaned, 'But I wanted to go to Fire-in-the-Hole first!'

'Me too,' Danny Gilbert chimed in.

'Grandfather's Mansion,' Jake repeated firmly. 'We'll work our way around the park to Fire-in-the-Hole.' His tone of voice brooked no opposition and the boys meekly gave in, setting off ahead in the direction of the general store. An eyebrow raised in amusement as Jake put a guiding hand on Tanya's elbow. 'What a pair!'

'I wondered if you knew what you were letting yourself in for when you suggested that John bring a friend along to Silver Dollar City,' she laughed.

'You didn't think *I* was going to take him through Fire-in-the-Hole, did you?' Jake grinned.

'I should have known there was a method to your madness.'

Her smile accented the already radiant glow in her face that had nothing to do with the warm June sun, nor with the fact that she looked very attractive in her slim-fitting blue slacks and the tightly woven lace blouse that hinted at the golden colour of her skin without revealing it. It was based on the warm friendliness of the man at her side and the easygoing relationship that had developed between them since the close of school and their more frequent outings with John.

'That Danny is a very curious boy.' Jake was watching with amusement as the two youngsters produced their tickets and entered the topsy-turvy fun house with gay abandon. 'I had the impression I was being interrogated on the ride here.'

'You were.' Her gold-flecked eyes danced with merriment as she met his curious glance. 'Danny Gilbert is the boy who had serious doubts that John had a father in Africa or that he had a father at all. Hence all the questions about lions and tigers and zebras.'

'Don't forget the elephants,' Jake reminded her with an amused shake of his head.

'And the giraffes. I think you let John down terribly when you told Danny that most of the animals were in game preserves,' Tanya scolded him with mock dismay.

'You should have warned me beforehand that

Danny was the instigator of the letter that brought me home. I could have made up a tall tale of a safari into the jungle.'

'I think John is quite satisfied just to have you home.'

Jake's eyes travelled lightly over her face. 'How about you? Are you glad I'm home?' There was a watchful stillness in his expression.

'There are moments when you're handy to have around,' Tanya replied, refusing to answer his question seriously. 'You're an excellent live-in baby-sitter for John.'

'It's nice to be useful,' he commented with a teasing smile, not pressing for any other kind of admission. 'Speak of the devil, here they come now.'

Danny and John burst from the side exit door with the same exuberance as when they had entered, dashing like a pair of whirlwinds towards Jake and Tanya.

'Where to next?' John asked in breathless excitement.

'The candy shop,' Tanya answered.

'We have a sweet tooth in the crowd,' Jake teased.

'Not really,' she demurred gaily. 'I like to watch them make it, though.'

Over a quarter of an hour later, the foursome walked out of the shop, all munching on a sample piece of freshly made peanut brittle.

'Can we go see the wooden Indians next?' Danny asked. At Jake's nod of agreement, he

130

grabbed hold of John's arm. 'Come on. Let's go over the swinging bridge!'

Jake and Tanya set out after them at a more leisurely pace. Two teenage girls came walking towards them, giggling behind their hands and glancing over their shoulders, not paying the slightest bit of attention to where they were going.

One girl would have walked right into Jake if he hadn't put his hands out to stop her. She glanced up at him in surprise, her face turning a brilliant shade of red as she mumbled a stammering 'Excuse me.'

'It was my pleasure,' Jake winked, a wide smile on his face as he released his hold on her shoulders.

Tanya knew by the dazed took on the girl's face that the Lassiter charm had made another conquest. She heard the awed exchanges after they had continued on their way and she smiled in secret agreement at the compliments they gave Jake.

'What's that smug smile for?' he asked, his gaze running possessively over her face.

'Oh, those girls thought you were very handsome,' she mocked, provocatively glancing at him out of the corner of her eyes, reaching out to put a trailing hand on the bridge railing. The boys were just ahead, their heads hanging over the railing as they gazed into the ravine below.

'Do you agree with their opinion?' he asked with lazy interest.

She pretended to study his face as though it hadn't already been implanted in her mind's eye. 'I think,' tilting her head to one side to get a better view of his artfully carved features, 'you're a bit too arrogant to be truly handsome.'

A low, rumbling sound of laughter followed her words as Jake reached out to enclose her waist with his hands. 'Tanya Lassiter, you're flirting with me,' he accused. Rolling waves of warmth spread out from where his hands touched her.

'I wasn't,' her breathy protest was enforced by her fingers moving out to touch the tanned flesh of his bare arms in an attempt to ward him off.

'You were, too, and you're going to have to pay the consequences,' he averred, his gaze centred on her parted lips.

'Jake, there are people watching.' She glanced around quickly and couldn't see a soul anywhere near them. 'And . . . and I don't see the boys.'

'If those are the only reasons you have for not wanting me to kiss you, I'll wait for a more opportune moment,' he agreed, flicking a finger over the pink colour in her cheek.

They caught up with the boys at the woodcarver's shop, lingered with the youngsters as they watched a woodcarver at work, strolled through the area where the carvings were for sale, and paused in front of the wooden Indian at the entrance door. It was every bit as tall as Tanya, dressed in buckskins and a feathered warbonnet, implacable and proud, his hands folded in front of him.

'How would you like to have him guarding the foyer at home?' Jake asked John, who was studiously studying every hand-carved detail.

'I think it would be great, but I bet Grandmother wouldn't,' the silken brown head nodded sagely.

'You're probably right there, John,' Jake agreed, ruffling the soft hair affectionately. He glanced at Tanya, an enigmatic expression on his face. 'I do envy that Indian.'

'Why?' A curious smile etched in her face.

'I don't have a wooden heart like he does.'

Her pulse responded to the softly worded statement, pounding at a furious pace at the base of her throat. He was only flirting with her as she had done with him, but it disturbed her more than she cared to have him know. Luckily the boys were there and she could transfer her attention to them and remove herself from the disturbing gleam in Jake's eyes.

'Do you want to visit the Flooded Mine next?' she asked, knowing she would be met by instant affirmation. Tanya turned a composed smile towards Jake. 'I'd suggest the glass-blowing factory, but I'm afraid they'd be like bulls in a china shop.'

'Oh, boy, the Flooded Mine!' Danny yelped.

'Are you two going to come along this time?' John asked, looking hopefully at his father.

Tanya was about to agree when Jake put a hand on her shoulder, his sudden touch stealing away her voice. 'No, you and Danny go by your-selves,' he commanded.

Minutes later Tanya stood near the fence pro-tecting the moat-surrounded, so-called Flooded Mine watching as John and Danny disappeared into the tunnel. Jake was standing directly be-hind her, the heat from his body almost as warm as the sun's rays.

'Do you?' he asked cryptically.

'Do I what?' She half-turned to look at him over her shoulder. The light breeze blew a lock of hair across her cheek which Jake gently pushed back behind her ear.

'Do you have a wooden heart?'

'Of course not,' Tanya laughed, trying to make his question a joke while her nerves vibrated from his nearness.

'Supposing I fell in love with you, what would you do?' Jake asked calmly. Her eyes widened in surprise overlaid with fear. 'Don't look so fright-ened,' he mocked. 'I didn't say I was, only sup-posing I was in love with you.'

She turned abruptly away from him, her gaze searching wildly about her for some avenue of escape, even as her heart palpitated at the over-powering thought. 'I never supposed any such thing, so I don't know what I would do,' she mur-mured.

'I don't know why you wouldn't suppose it,' Jake continued blandly. 'You're a beautiful and desirable woman. We've got along very well these last couple of months. I already know you're an excellent mother. You have a decidedly old-fashioned outlook on things which I admire and respect. In fact, you have most of the qualities I would want in a wife. A real wife, I'm talking about.'

'Now you're the one who's flirting with me,' she teased, but her legs were beginning to refuse to support her.

'Maybe,' he agreed smoothly. 'What I said is also the truth. Now that I'm home, I want to stay here. The idea of home and hearth and a pretty wife to bring me my slippers and paper is very appealing. When I look at John, I think it would be good for him to have a brother . . . maybe even a sister with tawny eyes and unusual streaked blonde hair.' His breath was stirring her hair with a devastating effect on her senses.

'Don't . . . don't talk that way,' Tanya breathed, starting to move away before his velvet words could wreak more havoc, but his hands closed over her shoulders, bringing them back against his chest.

'Why not?' he murmured near her ear. 'After these last few weeks, would you still find it so very hard to love me?'

'No . . . I mean, yes . . .' The nibbling caress on her ear was destroying all ability for coherent thought.

His low chuckle rippled over her. 'Make up your mind. Is it yes or no?'

'Please, Jake,' she gulped, moving determinedly away in a desperate need to put space between them. 'I can't think straight when you do that.'

'That's a step in the right direction,' he murmured with a lazy smile.

'It doesn't mean anything. Every human being responds to a caress,' she corrected quickly. Deprived of his touch, she was fighting the withdrawal pains attacking her heart. 'I like you. I think you're a good father. You're an attractive man as well. But I don't think I want to complicate my life by falling in love with you.'

The frown on his face was a mixture of curiosity and amusement. 'How would falling in love with me complicate your life? Surely it would simplify it, since you're already married to me.'

'You don't understand,' Tanya protested, finding herself caught in a trap of her own making.

'I'm trying to,' Jake answered patiently. 'Perhaps you could explain it to me.'

'No,' she shook her head in desperation, 'I don't think so.'

'Why not?' His gaze had become sharp and the hooded look was back in his eyes.

'I just don't want to,' Tanya shrugged helplessly. 'Not now anyway.'

'I'm not playing games with you, Tanya,' Jake said quietly. 'I'm deadly serious when I tell you I want to make our marriage work. It hasn't been easy, but lately we've been able to put the past behind us. Don't try to hang on to that old bitterness of the past. It will only sour the future.'

'I know,' she sighed, a wistfully sad look in her eyes when she met his gaze. 'But there are some things a person just can't forget, no matter how hard they try.'

'You've got to, Tanya,' he said grimly. 'You've got to, or else all this is in vain.'

'You said yourself, Jake, that it would take time. Wishing won't make it go away,' she murmured.

'Do you believe that we have a chance?' he asked softly. Tanya glanced up to see he had moved a step closer to her.

'Sometimes,' she breathed, gazing into his lazy, half-closed eyes. 'Sometimes I do.'

'I'm just going to have to change that "sometimes" into "most of the time",' he smiled, the confidence in his voice indicating that he could do it with a snap of his fingers.

'I wish you could.' Tanya lowered her chin only to have him capture it in his hand and raise it back up.

'All you have to do is meet me halfway. I've never asked you to do all the giving,' said Jake. 'But marriage isn't a fifty-fifty proposition, as some people say. It has to be one hundred per cent on both sides to be a success.'

'Have you ever considered that you might be asking too much from both of us?' whispering the chilling question that put such a cold finger of dread on her heart.

'Have you ever considered the possibility that you're making mountains out of molehills?' His teasing question was accompanied by a mockingly exasperated shake of his head. 'You can question something to death, you know. Let's take this whole thing as it comes and stop trying to rush the fences.'

'Blind faith in the future?' Tanya smiled.

'Don't you believe that I would guide you safely?' But he seemed to sense her unwillingness to reply to that question, knowing it would require an admission that she wasn't ready to make. Instead he reached out for her hand. 'Here come the boys. Prepare yourself for the onslaught. Fire-in-the-Hole is the next stop.'

Fire-in-the-Hole, Tree-top House, the Float Trip — they made all the rides except for the Steam Train. They stopped to watch the construction of a log cabin, candles being made, and a potter at his wheel.

At the spinning shop, a woman demonstrated the use of a spinning wheel to make wool into yarn and showed them the weasel used to measure yarn into skeins. Forty turns of the weasel's wheel equalled a skein. The woman pointed out the notched metal disc in the wheel, explaining that there were forty notches to save the pioneers from counting each revolution. On the fortieth turn, a block fell into place, preventing the wheel from turning. The woman smiled warmly, 'Or to quote the nursery rhyme — "pop goes the weasel",' to the delight of the crowd.

John was the one who signalled the end of their excursion through Silver Dollar City where unique rides were combined with exhibits of old-time crafts.

'I'm hungry, Mom,' he declared, an announcement that quickly brought agreement from Danny.

'So am I, *Mom*,' Jake added his laughing voice to the pleas of the two boys, his eyes twinkling at the rosy cheeks belonging to Tanya.

'One picnic lunch coming up,' she declared cheerfully trying to cover the attack of embarrassed shyness his teasing words had evoked.

When they were all in the car ready to leave, Jake turned to her. 'Where are we supposed to have this picnic?'

'Inspiration Point,' she suggested.

'Inspiration Point it is,' he agreed.

The picnic basket contained ample helpings of fried chicken, baked beans, and potato chips with the plastic plates and silverware. And there was potato salad, cole slaw and cider in the ice chest. It didn't take long for the hunger pangs to be satisfied.

'Let's go up to the top of the hill and see the statues,' John piped up the instant the food was cleared away.

Jake looked over at Tanya, tilting his brown head to one side. 'Are you game?' he asked. 'Or have you tackled enough hills for one day?'

'I'm never too tired to refuse the view from this hill,' she assured him, lightly accepting his outstretched hand.

'It's beautiful, isn't it?' Tanya commented, her

voice softly pitched. Even John and Danny stood in silence, the scene impressing them, too.

Jake's hand stole around her waist, drawing her into the shelter of his chest and arm. 'Geologists claim that these Ozark Hills are the oldest mountains or highlands on this Continent. It's amazing how after all these years they still manage to look untouched by civilization.'

'Dad.' John looked up, his face drawn into a quizzical frown. 'How old is the Trail That Is Nobody Knows How Old?'

'You've answered your own question,' Jake smiled. 'Nobody knows how old it is.'

'Why don't they?' he persisted.

'Well, when the first settlers came here in the late 1800s, the trail was here curving along below the Matthews place to Dewey Bald and on to the outside world miles away. Those settlers said the fur traders and trappers used it before them. The trappers said the French and Spanish explorers travelled over it, guided by the Indians who had used it before the explorers. And the Indians said the trail was there before them when the Old Ones walked the hills. So you see, it was named correctly — The Trail That Is Nobody Knows How Old.'

John nodded, and stood there gazing intently at the scene.

'He's an intelligent boy,' said Jake, lowering his voice so that his comment was for Tanya's ears alone.

'A bit too serious sometimes,' she added absently, enjoying the gentle rise and fall of his chest beneath her head as she stared dreamily at the panoramic view.

'Right now he looks like a normal, healthy boy to me,' Jake chuckled, bringing her gaze around to John. The moment of inactivity had passed and he and Danny had erupted into a boisterous game of tag. 'You worry about him too much, honey.' His lips brushed the top of her hair in an affectionate caress.

'I suppose I do,' she agreed ruefully, resisting the impulse to snuggle closer. 'But that comes from having to stretch yourself from one parent into two.'

'You don't have to do that any more.' His arm tightened, drawing her nearer.

She tilted her head back to look up at him, reeling a bit at the brightness in his eyes. 'I know I don't,' she said, letting the slow smile of happiness widen her mouth.

'One of these days,' Jake murmured, 'I'm going to accept that invitation written on your lips regardless of any people watching.'

A waft of radiant confusion coloured her face which she quickly turned away. She wondered if he felt the sudden leaping of her heart.

'Look, there's a persimmon tree over there.' She spoke to direct his attention away from her.

'We'll have to go persimmon and paw-paw picking this autumn after the first good frost,' Jake nodded.

'I'd like that.'

'You don't think we're planning too far ahead?' he whispered, nuzzling her ear playfully. Tanya drew back in surprise. 'It's too late!' Jake laughed. 'You've already committed yourself to going with me and I'm not going to let you back out. We have a date for this fall, so, my little honey, you'd better plan to stick around.'

'That's not fair,' she protested.

'All is fair,' he mocked.

Tanya would have pursued her argument if John hadn't come running towards them with Danny only a step behind him.

'Can I trade my pocket-knife to Danny for Harry? He said I could have him if I gave him my knife. Can I, please?' he urged.

'First of all, who is Harry?' Tanya asked with an indulgent smile.

'He's my pet —' Danny replied, sliding a sideways glance at John.

'Surely you don't want to give away your pet, do you?' Jake inquired, amusement and suspicion in the gaze that encompassed the pair.

'My mother says I have to get rid of it anyway,' Danny shrugged.

'Can I trade him my pocket-knife?'

'I don't know —' Tanya began, only to have Jake interrupt.

'Exactly what is Harry?'

'Exactly?' Danny repeated, shifting uncomfortably from one foot to the other. 'Harry is my pet . . . tarantula.'

'A spider?' A violent shudder quaked over

Tanya's shoulders and down her spine.

'Tarantulas don't hurt you, Mom,' John rushed in. 'They aren't poisonous. Dad told me so. He said the ones in the jungle are, but these around here don't hurt you when they bite you any more than a wasp sting hurts. They just crawl up your arm and things.'

'No, absolutely not!' she stated unequivocally.

'Ah, Mom, please,' John wheedled. 'I'd keep him outside.'

'Your mother said no, John,' Jake stepped in. 'There won't be any more discussion about it, all right?'

His head bobbed glumly in agreement as he scuffed his shoes in the gravel. 'Come on, Danny,' he grumbled.

As the pair trotted away, Tanya shivered again and began vigorously rubbing her arms. 'I can feel that horrible thing crawling on me right now,' she shuddered.

'Poor Little Miss Muffet,' Jake teased. 'Are you afraid of spiders?'

'I have a terrible, unreasoning fear of them,' she declared fervently. 'It doesn't matter how harmless they are. Even a daddy-long-legs can send me standing on a chair. I know it's silly, but I can't seem to help it.'

'Well, you can be glad John asked before he made the trade. The poor boy would have been minus a pocket-knife and a spider the second you found out about it,' Jake grinned.

'I can be thankful for that,' she agreed, another

smaller shudder shaking her shoulders.

'Or you could keep me around as your official spider-slayer,' he suggested with a decidedly tongue-in-cheek expression.

'That's the best proposition you've made,' Tanya laughed.

'With a little encouragement,' his eyes made a slow, deliberate appraisal of her curved figure, 'I'd make a few more.'

'I think. . . .' His disturbing look made it difficult to speak. 'I think it's time we took Danny home.'

'You're very adept at dodging the issue, aren't you?' Jake mocked, but drew no reply from Tanya. 'Very well, we'll call it a day. A very enjoyable day.'

'Yes, it was,' she agreed softly.

That day spent almost entirely in each other's company seemed to put their relationship one plateau higher than before. Jake paid more little attentions to her, greeting her specifically when he came home and not including her any more in a general greeting, holding her hand when she was standing or sitting next to him. A lot of little things that were not significant on their own, but very special when looked at as a whole. Tanya could almost believe that he wanted to love her as a person, not as the mother of his child.

It was becoming more and more easy to turn her face to his for the goodnight kiss that was slowly becoming a habit. He was always gentle and controlled, never demanding more than she was willing to give. Yet her reticence, born of fear, increased in the same proportion as her love for Jake. The rapport between them was bitter-sweet agony, made all the more painful by the shattering secret that kept pushing itself forward every time she thought she and Jake had a chance for happiness together.

Perhaps if she had told him at the beginning, Tanya thought to herself as she idly plucked at the cord around the cushion of the redwood lounge chair. But where was the beginning? She only knew she had kept it from him too long for Jake to understand and forgive her.

The patio door to the house slid open, drawing a casual glance from Tanya. Her eyes widened fractionally as Sheila Raines walked confidently towards her looking vitally attractive in a trouser suit of crimson red.

'Hi,' she greeted Tanya cheerfully. 'Is Jake around?'

'No, he hasn't come home yet.' A stillness crept into Tanya's expression, instantly on guard at Sheila's familiar tone.

Red lips pursed in a grimacing pout. 'That's a pity. He said he was coming home early today, and I hoped to catch him here. Do you know how long he'll be?'

'No, I don't.' There was a condescending arch of Tanya's brows. She refused to let Sheila know that Jake hadn't confided his plans to her. 'Would you like to wait for him?'

'No,' Sheila glanced at her diamond-studded

watch. 'I really have to dash off.' A regretful sigh shuddered through the very feminine form. 'I did so want to see him this afternoon.'

'Was it important?' Tanya asked archly, disliking the possessive ring in the girl's voice. 'I could give him a message for you.'

'Would you?' The voice gushed as though Tanya were doing her an enormous favour. 'I could telephone him later on, of course, but I don't like to intrude on the time he spends with his son.'

'That's very thoughtful of you,' Tanya murmured, her temper seething closer to the surface.

'There's been a mix-up in the time we're supposed to be at the Country Club. Tell him it's one o'clock Saturday instead of two.'

'Saturday at one. I'll give him the message,' Tanya nodded grimly.

'Thanks,' Sheila purred, turning as if to leave only to stop and add, 'I almost forgot. I looked at that piece of property he was interested in buying. Tell him that it just won't do at all. It's practically inaccessible. What lakefront there is on it is a mass of barely submerged trees and the view is disgustingly bland. I'll give him all the rest of the details on Saturday. Maybe then we'll have time to go look at the property together.'

Tanya was too angry to trust herself to speak. Jake had never mentioned one word to her that he was looking at land for sale in the area. Had these last months together been a trick intended to lull her into believing Jake cared while he continued to carry on his affair with Sheila? Sheila's unexpected visit had made the affirmative answer to that question very apparent.

Something in her expression must have betrayed the doubts and jealousy in her heart, because the brunette's dark eyes glittered with complacent satisfaction as she waved goodbye and started for the patio door.

'I'll tell Patrick you said "hello",' she called cheerily.

CHAPTER EIGHT

Sheila had been gone only a half hour when Tanya heard a car in the drive. Since Sheila had told her that Jake was coming home early today, she guessed that it had to be him. The anger that had seethed to the boiling point demanded she rush out to confront him with her knowledge of his affair with Sheila, but she remained in the lounge chair, the bitterness in her eyes hidden by sunglasses.

It was several moments before the patio door opened and closed and Tanya glanced up to see Jake carrying two iced drinks in his hands. His gaze slid over her bare legs to the white shorts and the blue polka-dot top. In other circumstances his raking gaze would have disturbed her. Now she knew its falseness.

'Cold nectar for the sun goddess,' Jake mocked, handing her one of the glasses as he continued to stand above her.

That lazy smile pierced her guard and sent her pulse leaping. Tanya suppressed a shudder over how completely she had succumbed to his virile charm.

'I hadn't expected you home so soon,' she

murmured, allowing only a saccharine smile to tug the corners of her mouth.

'Mother stopped into the office this noon to have lunch with Dad. She mentioned she'd dropped John off at one of his friend's house for a birthday party. I knew I wouldn't have a better opportunity to be alone with my wife, so I persuaded Mother to do some shopping and drive Dad home later when she'd picked up John.'

Tanya rose to her feet on the opposite side of the chair where Jake was standing. Bitterness rose like a sickening ball in her throat, with the knowledge that once such a statement would have elated her.

'I had a visitor this afternoon,' she announced casually, minutely examining his face through the protective darkness of her glasses.

'Oh? Who was it?'

'Sheila Raines.' Her identification brought a brief moment of guarded stillness to his face as his eyes narrowed to study her marble smooth face.

'What did she want?' His tone of voice sounded curious but indifferent.

'Actually she didn't come to see me. It was you she was looking for.' Tanya was glad he didn't try to look surprised. In fact she found malicious pleasure in the grimness of his expression.

'Did she say why?'

'She did leave a message,' Tanya nodded, glancing down at her drink, then she tilted her head back at a challenging angle. 'I'm to tell you to meet her at one o'clock instead of two at the Country Club on Saturday. She didn't say which one, but I'm sure you know.' His blue eyes glittered with ominous coldness at the biting sarcasm in her voice. 'And she also said she looked at that piece of property you were interested in and — in her words — "it won't do at all", something about submerged trees in the lake and bad roads. She said the two of you could look over some other property on Saturday.'

'I intended to tell you about that this afternoon.' The muscle twitching in his jaw indicated the tight check on his temper.

'Well, now you don't have to tell me, do you?' she mocked sweetly. 'I already know.'

'You only know the part that Sheila told you, and you seem to have put the wrong construction on that,' he snapped.

'Oh, spare me the explanations!' Tanya cried angrily, releasing the constricting hold she had placed on her temper. 'I have no doubt that you can twist things around to make it sound as if you've done nothing wrong.'

'I haven't. Not the way you mean,' Jake bit out.

'How terribly self-righteous you must have felt that day you saw me with Patrick! You told me you couldn't tolerate being deceived,' she laughed bitterly. 'That very day Patrick told me you were still seeing Sheila, but I refused to take him seriously. I accepted your word that you were going to try as hard as I to make our marriage work. I should have remembered how worthless your word was!'

A string of muttered imprecations came from Jake as he covered the distance between them with the swiftness of a striking cobra. 'You are going to listen to me!' he growled, grabbing her shoulders and giving them a savage shake.

But Tanya was just as quick to twist free, her anger pumping strength into her body that she didn't normally possess.

'I've listened to your lies for the last time!'

'You're doing the very same thing I did. You are accusing me and convicting me without even waiting for my explanation. Surely I've earned the right to a little of your trust!' His tall form loomed near her, formidable in his leashed fury.

'How gullible I must seem to you,' Tanya declared, bitter shame bringing tears of anguish to her glittering gold eyes. 'How many times I've believed you! And every time you've made a fool of me. Now you expect me to believe you again when you make up some innocent little tale to explain away the intimate relationship Sheila made so clear.' Jake opened his mouth to speak, but her hand forestalled his words. 'No, don't say anything. You never once said you were giving Sheila up — in fact, you avoided the answer the only time I asked, so it really was only a white lie. Maybe I deceived myself. It doesn't matter any more now that I know the truth.'

'But you don't know the truth! You won't listen to the truth!' His husky voice was embedded with angry exasperation.

151

The shrill ring of the telephone sounded from inside the house. Jake determinedly ignored it. 'You'd better answer that,' Tanya murmured coldly. 'Sheila said she might call later.'

His gaze was harsh and ruthlessly thorough as it swept over the implacably firm expression on her face. The line of his mouth was taut and grim as he turned away to stride into the house.

After his departure, the anger that had sustained her began to ebb away and Tanya could have wept at the unbearable pain in her heart. Without the support of her avenging rage, she sagged weakly against the patio railing, knowing she had a few minutes' respite to regain her strength before Jake returned. Or so she thought, until the patio door slid open.

'Tanya, come in here,' he ordered in an uncompromising voice. She didn't even glance in his direction as she moved her tawny hair in a negative movement. 'Come in here or I'll come and drag you in!'

Something in his voice told her he would do that very thing if she refused him again, so she walked slowly towards him, keeping her shoulders squared and her gaze averted from the harshness of his. She didn't attempt to shake free of the hand that closed over her arm and led her forcibly towards the telephone in the foyer, the receiver off the hook lying on top of the small stand.

Jake picked it up and spoke into the mouthpiece. 'Repeat what you just told me, Dad.' Then he thrust it against Tanya's ear.

'Repeat it?' J. D. Lassiter's voice echoed with surprise. 'All I said was that the meeting for the executives and area engineers of the firm was changed from Saturday at two o'clock to one o'clock. It's an informal meeting with the wives invited, so be sure to let Tanya know. She'll want to make arrangements for a babysitter for John. What's so difficult to remember about that?'

The rigidity went out of her body, carried away by the shuddering sigh that acknowledged the grievous error of her accusation.

'Thanks, Dad,' said Jake, taking the receiver back. Tanya could feel his hard gaze studying her tightly closed eyes.

'Wait a minute,' said J.D., his far-away voice carrying to Tanya's hearing as well. 'Your mother just reminded me that Sheila left a list of unimproved land for sale on my desk. I won't be coming to the office tomorrow, so be sure to pick it up from my secretary. I never believed she'd actually get her real estate licence,' he laughed. 'But she's a hard enough woman to be a success at selling. Beauty and ruthless perseverance are a potent combination.'

This time Tanya's eyes flashed open, rounded in shock and pain as she stared into Jake's implacably grim face. Anger still glittered in his blue eyes, the metallic sheen of tempered steel. He was speaking into the telephone, but she was too stunned to hear what he was saying.

'I'm sorry, Jake, I'm very sorry,' she whispered,

153

taking a frightened step backwards before pivoting to stumble clumsily outside.

She couldn't face him, not now, not after she had so wrongly misjudged him. Her mumbled apology couldn't adequately make up for all the horrible things she had said. As she sped down the path leading from the patio to the lake, she knew she should have kept her doubts in abeyance until she had heard Jake's explanation. But her jealousy ran so deep that she probably wouldn't have believed him even then. And Jake guessed that.

Tears spilled over her cheeks, blurring her vision until she couldn't see where she was going. At the layered shelf of rocks a few yards away from the lake's edge, she stopped, her feet crumpling beneath her as she sagged to the ground to weep freely. Unconsciously she pushed away the sharp, loose rocks that jabbed into her body. The grief and misery and frustration that had been building up over the last seven years were released in a torrent of racking sobs that shook her body until there weren't any tears left.

As the last shuddering sobs faded away, she pressed a hand to her temple and leaned back against the rocks to stare at the brilliant blue summer sky. She felt like a lost child who had run away and only wanted to find his way back again. The numbness began to leave as a fly landed lightly on her arm, then buzzed away. Irritatingly it came back to flit around her face until she moved her hand to flick it away.

Something brushed her leg once, then again. Tanya leaned forward to rid herself of the fly — and horror rose in her throat as she stared at the large hairy body of a tarantula. Basically a night creature, the scattering of loose rocks had disturbed his burrow and now he was preparing to cross the obstacle in his path — her legs. Tanya was too terrified to move, frozen by the sight of the mammoth spider. But when it began to crawl on to her petrified legs, she screamed.

In her terror, she didn't recognize that she was calling Jake's name over and over again. Nor did she hear the sound of footsteps racing towards her. The only thing that registered was the tanned hand brushing the spider off her leg and the pair of arms that reached down and pulled her to her feet. Then she was crushed against a muscular chest, the arms wrapped around her, a hand stroking her hair as she gasped in shuddering breaths against the warm body.

'It's okay. You're all right now,' a soothing voice whispered in her ear.

'Jake, Jake,' she moaned.

'I'm here. Take it easy now, nothing's going to happen. The spider's gone,' he assured her quietly. 'There's nothing to be afraid of any more.'

'I can still feel him crawling on me,' she shivered, her voice still trembling from the depths of her unreasoning fear. Although it was impossible, Jake seemed to draw her closer against him, and her arms circled his waist to cling tightly to him.

'Are you all right now?' he asked, gently tucking her hair behind her ear.

Tanya nodded numbly, keeping her face pressed against the reassuring solidness of his chest. 'I know it's silly to be so frightened, but I can't help it,' she murmured. 'Hold me a little while longer, please, Jake.'

'As long as you want,' he agreed with a hint of a smile in his voice.

It was several more minutes before Tanya reluctantly untangled her arms from around his waist. Her legs still felt weak and unsteady, but enough of the shock had worn away to make her feel self-conscious over the way she was clinging to him.

'I think I'm all right now,' she murmured, keeping her eyes downcast as he let her move to arm's length.

'Have you forgiven me?' Jake asked softly as he caressed her warm cheeks with his hand.

'F . . . for what?'

'For not being here in my official role as spider-slayer,' he teased.

An embarrassed laugh slipped from her mouth. 'Of course. I thought you were talking about Sheila.'

'We won't talk about her now,' he said, tilting her chin as he ran his thumb along her lower lip and gazed deeply into her gold-flecked eyes. 'You aren't up to the discussion I want to have.'

'I want you to know that I realize how very wrong I was when I wouldn't let you explain earlier,' Tanya persisted.

'I told you we'd discuss it later.' Mock exasperation beamed from his face.

'I know.' Like a child, she needed the reassurance of his forgiveness. 'But I had to tell you how badly I feel.'

'You're stubborn,' he smiled slowly, pulling her gently into his arms again.

His warm, moist mouth covered hers, moving sensually against it until her lips parted in response. But when her hands moved up to his neck to draw him into a deeper kiss, Jake halted them with his own hands, slowly raising his mouth from hers.

'Your apology is accepted.' Thick lashes acted as a smoky veil to conceal the smouldering fire in his gaze. 'Now, do you want to walk up to the house or shall I carry you?'

'I'd better walk,' Tanya declared breathlessly, knowing that if she were cradled in his arms the way she was feeling at this moment, she would be shamelessly caressing him.

'You don't feel safe in my arms any more, hm?' he mocked, and chuckled when she didn't answer.

He kept a steadying hand on her arm as they travelled over the rocky path back to the house. Inside, he escorted her to her room.

'Go in there and freshen up,' he ordered. 'We'll have a talk when you're done.'

'What talk?' she asked, but he had already gently shoved her into the room and was closing the door.

Was it about Sheila? Tanya wondered, then shrugged. She was too drained of emotion at the moment to think straight. The thought of a brisk shower to chase away the last creeping sensation of the tarantula was very inviting.

She had just towelled herself dry and slipped on her ivory satin robe when there came a knock on her door. 'Come in,' she called, untying the ribbon that bound her hair on top of her head, shaking the damp tendrils loose with her fingers.

'You look much better,' Jake declared, pausing for a moment in the doorway, his tall figure imposing itself in the suddenly small room. He walked on in, handing her a tall, frosted glass of lemonade. 'There aren't any shadows of fear in your eyes now.'

Tanya couldn't keep the sudden light from springing into them when she looked into his ruggedly handsome face. 'I must have made a complete fool of myself,' she murmured, turning away to take a sip of the drink, then set it on the dressing table to begin brushing her hair. 'I wish I could get over that childish fear of spiders. But those tarantulas are so grotesquely menacing.'

Her composure had returned and she was grateful for it. There was a rustle of paper near the bed. As she glanced behind her, she noticed for the first time the roll of blue paper Jake had carried under his arm.

'What's that?' she asked, watching curiously as he unrolled it on the bed.

'Come and look.'

He stood quietly beside her as she stared down at the rectangular drawing. 'It's a blueprint of a house,' she said.

'Not of a house,' he corrected. 'It's our home.' His gaze blandly met her startled glance. 'Since Sheila insisted on telling you that I was interested in buying some property, I decided I might as well tell you the rest.'

'What do you mean — our home?' Tanya breathed.

'Aren't you getting tired of living with my parents?' he mocked. 'Not that I don't love them dearly, but wouldn't you like a home of your own?'

'Of course, but —' she hesitated, recognizing the implication of his words.

'Then you'd better give me your opinion of this layout. There may be something you want to change.' Jake didn't give her an opportunity to comment as he pointed out the location of the living room and family room, the kitchen and the proposed location of its appliances, the bathrooms, and the bedrooms, showed her where the fireplace would be and the washroom area. 'Do you like it?' he concluded.

'It's beautiful,' she murmured, 'but —' Her voice trailed away as she shook her head to keep from falling under the enchantment of the dream house.

'What's the matter, honey?' His hand raised her chin so he could look more closely into the troubled expression in her eyes. 'Don't you think it's about time we have some privacy in our marriage?'

She was suddenly tense, too afraid to speak and equally afraid not to. She stared at him, drinking in the artfully carved features, knowing how very much she loved him. 'Oh, Jake,' she moaned helplessly.

Instantly he drew her into his arms, his mouth passionately raining kisses over her face as though every perfect feature was precious to him. Her heart pounded wildly against her ribs at his touch. He nibbled at her ear lobe, then sent an erotic trail of fire along her neck as he explored the sensitive cord.

'I've wanted to do this for so long,' he murmured huskily into her ear, his breath fanning the flames already racing through her.

The satin robe was like a second skin covering her nakedness as his hands caressingly moulded her to his lean body, sliding over her hips and up to her shoulders. All the while his mouth sensually explored the hollow of her throat, pushed aside the satin to kiss her shoulders until Tanya was a churning mass of desire. With a tortured cry, she captured his face in her hands and brought it to her mouth, letting him take it captive with his own.

For long moments, Jake ravaged her lips, bruising them with the fierceness of his passion, parting them roughly so he could know the full response of his lovemaking. Her fingers twined themselves in his hair as she moaned his name against his lips. There was wild joy in their intense hunger for each other's caress, a hunger that went beyond the bounds of the physical to a joining of their souls.

Reluctantly Jake pulled his lips from hers, roughly dragging his kiss along her face to the top of her hair. 'You don't know the self-control I've exercised to keep myself from making love to you like this before now.' His ragged breathing and his voice that was raw with desire only confirmed how completely Tanya's response had aroused him.

Her fingers ran ecstatically over his shoulders and arms, glorying in the muscles that swelled to bind her tighter in his embrace. Then she directed them to the open collar of his shirt, pushing it aside to kiss the hollow of his throat above the dark hair on his chest.

'Kiss me, Jake,' she commanded in a husky whisper as her mouth moved upwards to the strong chin.

'Tanya,' he groaned, resisting the pull of her hands that would have brought his mouth down on hers again. His eyes glittered on her parted lips. 'I want more than kisses from you.'

His gaze moved from the tempting invitation of her mouth to search her eyes for the answer to his unasked question. The advantage was all Jake's. If he had chosen to possess her, Tanya wouldn't have resisted. Now he was giving her a choice and fear sliced through her heart with the killing blow of a machete.

With a gasping sob of pain, she pivoted in the arms that held her in a tender but not confining embrace. Bitter tears burned her eyes. She felt his strong arms circle her waist and pull her against his chest. She was glad her back was to him and he couldn't see the misery and pain in her eyes.

'Don't be frightened, darling.' His mouth moved over her hair so that his velvet-rough voice whispered near her ear. 'It isn't just sexual desire I feel, although heaven knows I want you desperately.'

'Oh, Jake!' His name was a pleading cry of protest drawn achingly from her heart. It was not his touch that she feared, but his anger.

'Hush, my beloved,' he murmured, tightening his arms so she was moulded more firmly to his lean muscular body. 'You're entitled to the words. We both need them to wipe away the last of the bitterness.'

'Jake, I —'

'Don't talk. Just listen,' he scolded her tenderly. 'I love you. Maybe I always have. I don't know. I only know that I'm in love with you now, more deeply than I thought a human being was capable of feeling.'

A moan of intense longing escaped her lips as she sagged weakly against him, knowing her own love was as strong as his. 'Don't say any more, Jake, please,' she begged, wishing only to have this moment last for an eternity.

There was a moment of hesitation and Tanya

162

sensed that Jake wanted action to take over where his words had left off.

'Let me finish, darling,' he demanded huskily. 'Because after this moment I never want to bring up the past again.' He drew a deep, shuddering breath. 'I didn't come home because of that letter you sent me. I used it as an excuse. Not that John wasn't a factor, too, because he was. I wanted to see my son. But more I wanted to see my wife, that beautiful woman in the photograph. You, Tanya. The woman who had haunted me for seven years with the golden rays of sunlight in her hair and eyes.'

There was a bittersweet song in her heart. Perhaps their love was strong enough to overcome the anger and hostility of the past and enable him to understand why she had deceived him all these years.

'First you must understand that my brother and I were very close. We were more than brothers. I don't remember telling you I would come back that night at the fair, but I intended to — until Jamie was killed.' Tanya could feel the pain in his voice and her heart cried for his loss. 'He was so young, Tanya, with so much of his life ahead of him. I became terribly cynical and bitter. What memory I retained of that shy, sunshine girl I met became tainted by those emotions. Then when I saw you that day, more beautiful than I remembered, I cursed myself for not looking for you before, especially when I saw the baby in your arms. And that cold contempt in your eyes unnerved me. I knew you wanted me to go away and leave you alone, but I couldn't. That's why I pretended to take such an interest in the baby.'

His arms tightened about her as he rocked her gently against him, as if it would ease the pain in both their hearts.

'I'll never forget that first wave of shock that went through me when you said — Don't you recognize him? He's your son! At first I thought you were lying, that you'd found out about the relative wealth of the Lassiter family and wanted it for your illegitimate baby. I wasn't convinced even when you showed me the crooked little finger, the Lassiter birthmark. Not until later when I went to that squalid apartment where you were living did I accept the fact that he was my son, even if I couldn't remember the act of conception. My darling, can you ever forgive me for that?' he whispered.

'There's nothing to forgive,' she answered fervently, trying to turn to face him, but his arms held her where she was.

'When I asked you at your apartment if he was really my son, I can still remember that light shining in your eyes when you confirmed it again. In that moment I knew you weren't lying, that you weren't capable of lying.' His mouth moved along her neck. 'That's the one thing that's stood out in our marriage — your honesty. It was one of the first things I loved about you. It became the foundation of my love for you.'

'Oh, no, Jake, no,' Tanya groaned. Her heart that had been singing so joyously sank with sickening swiftness. The room reeled in front of her eyes as she wished the ground would open up and swallow her.

'I don't blame you for hating me at first,' Jake murmured. 'I did force you to marry me. I can't even be sure now if I did it to have my son or to have you as my wife. I only know that I despised myself for the degradation you must have suffered because of me. Every time you looked at me I was reminded of why you loathed me. You didn't drive me away, darling, I drove myself away. None of this was your fault. The blame is strictly mine.' There was a moment of hesitation as he gently squeezed her waist. 'You do see why I had to tell you all this, don't you, darling? You've been so honest with me that I had to do the same.'

Honest! Honest! The word kept taunting her like a sarcastic jeer. There wasn't any way she could tell him the truth now. Her supposed honesty was the one thing he admired about her. She couldn't destroy it or it would destroy his love for her.

'Why? Why did you have to tell me all this?' she sobbed, wrenching herself free from his arms. 'Don't you see it doesn't matter?'

'Darling, what's the matter with you?' The surprised and gentle concern in his voice only increased the pain.

'Oh, Jake, Jake!' Her head moved from side to

side in anguish. There was only one way out of this situation. He would hate her for it, but not nearly as much as he would if he found out the truth. 'Please, I want a divorce.'

'A divorce?' he repeated in disbelief, taking a step to erase the distance between them. His gaze was staring holes into her back. 'Is this some kind of a joke?'

'No, it's not a joke. I want a divorce.'

His hands closed over her shoulders, spinning her around to stare into her face. 'I just told you I love you! Are you trying to tell me that you don't love me?' he demanded angrily. 'Is that what you're saying?'

'I'm saying I want a divorce,' she answered more firmly, not able to meet the piercing regard of his eyes. 'Isn't that answer enough?'

'No, dammit! It isn't!' His fingers dug punishingly into the soft flesh of her upper arms. 'I'm not so inexperienced that I don't know when a woman wants me, and I know that a moment ago you wanted me as badly as I wanted you. You aren't a promiscuous woman.' The angry and confused expression on his face made Tanya's heart weep with pain. 'I know you love me. Admit it!'

'Stop it, Jake.' Her hands moved to his chest, trying to push herself away as he pulled her to him.

'I want an explanation!' One hand moved to the small of her back, arching her against his hips, while the other hand wound its fingers in her hair, twisting her head up towards his.

'You're hurting me,' she whispered, frightened by the cruel line of his mouth.

'I love you,' he growled, angry fires leaping in his eyes. 'I'll make you love me!'

He swung her into his arms, warding off the futile efforts of her hands to prevent him as he carried her to the bed. The blueprints were brushed aside before he dropped her on to the blue satin coverlet. The rough handling loosened the sash around her waist and the robe opened to show the tanned length of her legs. As her hand reached down in a frightened effort to cover herself, his fingers closed over her wrists, thrusting her backwards on to the bed while the full weight of his body pressed down on her.

His gaze was hard and alien as he stared into her face, without the seductive light that usually disturbed her. His head came down to capture her mouth, but Tanya twisted her head away.

'You were anxious enough for my kisses before,' he jeered, manoeuvring her hands until both wrists were held by one hand and he used the other to drag her face roughly around.

'Please, Jake, don't do this,' she whispered in a trembling voice. 'It won't change anything. I'll still want a divorce. Please, Jake, please!'

'I don't believe you,' he said coldly.

Tears gathered in the corners of her eyes. 'I haven't the strength to stop you, Jake.'

He stared down at her for a long moment. 'Damn you!' he muttered savagely as he broke free from the pleading look in her eyes and rolled off of her on to the floor. A shuddering sob moved through her as his footsteps carried him away from the bed. The door of her bedroom opened, then closed with a resounding slam.

'Oh, Jake, I love you,' Tanya sobbed into her pillow.

CHAPTER NINE

There was a lot of door-slamming in the course of the next days as Jake refused to be in the same room with Tanya. A brooding anger followed him like a dark cloud wherever he went until even John was hesitant to approach him lest he should feel the sharp side of his father's tongue. Tanya wondered if he even slept, because she could hear the restless pacing at night coming from the room across the hall.

The blue circles under her own eyes were evidence of her insomnia. Countless hours she lay awake staring at the ceiling wishing she could cross the hall and admit her love. But she didn't. Jake would never understand. So she suffered through the sleepless nights and the reproachful glances from Julia that plainly placed the blame for her son's departure before breakfast and his return after the evening meal on Tanya's shoulders. J.D. was the only one who looked at her with anything resembling sympathy. Yet he too seemed a bit grim and accusing.

Poor John was the one who was suffering the most. The hostile atmosphere in the house was something he hadn't experienced before. Danny

Gilbert had asked him to spend the night at his house and Tanya had agreed — somewhat reluctantly, it was true, because she selfishly wanted him around her to deflect as much of her attention as possible from Jake.

She was on her way to John's room to make sure all the necessities for an overnight stay had been packed when she passed Jake's doorway and glanced in. Her steps faltered, then stopped. Jake was standing in front of a mirror patiently tying a silver and blue striped tie to complement the perfectly tailored grey summer suit he was wearing. The elegant suit seemed to accent the cynical, world-weary hardness of his chiselled features. Tanya hadn't even known he was home yet and it looked as though he were getting ready to leave. His flint-hard eyes caught her reflection in the mirror.

'Are you going out?' she asked, feeling the need to say something since he had noticed her standing there.

'Yes.'

'Danny Gilbert asked John to spend the night with him.'

'So?' His eyes flicked over her reflection as he secured the tie clasp to his shirt.

'I thought perhaps you could take him,' Tanya suggested, not really sure why she was saying it at all except to have an excuse to talk to Jake a little while longer.

'Can't anyone else take him?' he asked coldly.

'Well, yes, of course,' she fumbled. 'But John

would like it if you took him. He doesn't quite understand why you're so seldom home now, and when you are, you're always going off by yourself.'

'Maybe you should enlighten him,' he jeered, turning so no mirror would reduce the effect of his contemptuous glare.

'Jake, please!' Tanya averted her eyes from the freezing disdain of his look.

'Please what?' he snapped bitterly. 'What do you expect of me? Am I supposed to say "Sorry, old gal, that it didn't work" and go my merry way? A man has only two things he can give a woman, Tanya — his love and his name. You're rejecting both! And you don't even have the decency to give me an explanation.' His mouth curled with disgust.

Not one word crossed her lips, although a thousand flooded from her mind. Her chin trembled as she murmured a very weak, 'I'm sorry,' and crossed the hallway to her room. Moments later his striding footsteps could be heard in the hall signalling his departure.

Somehow Tanya dried the tears his embittered words had aroused and recovered a sufficient amount of composure to enable her to drive John to the Gilbert house. On her return, she avoided entering the house, choosing to circle it to arrive at the patio in the rear. It didn't matter that Julia would probably want her help in the kitchen to prepare the evening meal. She needed to be alone.

She walked to the railing and stared absently at the glasslike surface of the lake shimmering beyond the trees. Tears of self-pity stung her eyes as she suddenly felt so sorry for herself at the mess she had made of her life. She made no attempt to wipe the dampness from her cheeks, feeling entitled to shed a few tears on her behalf.

'I didn't know anyone was out here,' J.D.'s smooth voice sounded behind her, causing her to turn with a start. 'You're crying, child,' he murmured sympathetically.

Tanya quickly wiped her face with the back of her hand. 'It's nothing,' she shrugged.

'Here,' he said, handing her the drink he held in his hand. 'You look more in need of this than I am. Take a hefty swallow.' She did as she was ordered, choking on the potent liquor in the process. 'Burns all the way down, doesn't it?' he smiled. 'But it momentarily revives you.'

'Thanks,' she said huskily, her throat still feeling the scorching effect as she started to hand the glass back.

'No.' He waved it off. 'You might need another dose. You and Jake have had another quarrel, haven't you?'

'More than a quarrel, I'm afraid,' she nodded, taking a deep breath to fight the shooting pain Jake's name caused.

'There couldn't be much doubt about that. He's been like an elephant with a toothache, snapping at everybody.' Tanya could feel his speculating gaze move over her face. 'You're in

172

love with my son, aren't you?'

She darted him a quick glance, but neither confirmed nor denied it. She couldn't. She didn't think J.D. would accept her lie that she wasn't in love with Jake and there was too much chance of the truth getting back to Jake.

'You'd rather not say, is that it?' J.D. chuckled. 'Surely you know that he's in love with you?'

'Yes,' she admitted in a tight voice.

'Would you consider me a nosey in-law if I asked what the quarrel was about?' His expression was friendly and warm when Tanya glanced at him.

She met his eyes squarely. 'I asked Jake for a divorce.'

One dark brow shot up in surprise. 'Why?'

'Personal reasons,' Tanya hedged.

'May I ask you another personal question?'

'What's that?' She couldn't keep from tilting her chin at a slightly defiant angle.

'Does Jake know that you aren't John's mother?'

The glass slipped from her hand and shattered into a hundred fragments on the patio floor. Icy fear held her in its paralysing grip.

'Obviously he doesn't,' J.D. said dryly.

'H— how . . . did you know?' she gasped, her hand slipping up to her throat in an oddly protective gesture.

'Let's say I wasn't as willing as my son to believe that this strange girl we'd never seen or heard of before was what she professed to be, and more important, whether the baby was really my grandchild. As far as I was concerned there was a very real possibility that you were only passing the boy off as Jake's son. Jake wouldn't discuss it with me except to admit that the baby had been born before you two were married. So I did some checking on my own.' His eyes looked kindly at her. 'Why was it that Jake never asked to see John's birth certificate?'

'He did once,' Tanya breathed, unable to believe any of this was really happening. 'But I didn't show it to him.'

'You can imagine my shock and anger when I saw that the birth certificate listed your sister as John's mother,' J.D. said with a rueful smile.

'Why didn't you confront me or Jake with your discovery?'

'You were legally married to Jake. No, I hinted a few times in my letters to him that there might be something he didn't know, but he wrote back that John was his son. I guessed from that that he knew the truth. By then,' he sighed, 'I could already see how very much you loved the boy, as if he were really your own.'

'When did you find out that Jake didn't know?' she whispered.

'That time I persuaded him to come home. I asked him one night about your sister, and he said he'd never met her.'

'He was drunk,' Tanya murmured. All the bitterness was gone and only sadness was in its place. 'He couldn't remember anything about that night except meeting me.'

'Why didn't you tell him the truth then, Tanya?' he asked quietly.

'Because he said he wanted his son.' She swallowed back the lump in her throat. 'And I knew that because he was John's father, with the Lassiter wealth and name to back him up, I didn't have a chance of keeping John. I loved John. Deanna, my sister, never got to hold him once. She came down with pneumonia in the hospital and died. I took care of him. He was my baby and Jake would have taken him away from me!'

She broke into sobs and found herself being drawn into her father-in-law's arms where he patted her shoulders and comforted her.

'I understand, child,' he soothed. As the last of the sobs faded away, he handed her his linen handkerchief. 'And now you're afraid to tell Jake what you did.'

Tanya nodded, blowing her nose gently in his handkerchief. 'Yes. He'd hate me for it.' A blankness swept over her face as if she were beyond feeling. 'He said I was honest, that I always told the truth. How can I tell him that I've been living a lie for seven years?'

'I'm afraid you have to.'

'I couldn't,' she shuddered.

'My dearest daughter-in-law,' J.D. said gently, lifting her chin with his finger, 'my son couldn't be more hurt or angered than he is right now because you rejected him. Do you really believe he's going to hate you more for telling him the truth?'

'I suppose not,' she murmured. 'I just don't know if I can face him, or if he'll even talk to me.'

'I'll arrange to have him come to my study to-morrow night at seven o'clock. I'll act as a referee for the first few minutes,' J.D. suggested.

'Maybe . . . maybe it would be better if you didn't tell him I was going to meet him there. He might not come if he knows he's to meet me.'

'You may be right,' he smiled. 'Jake can be as stubborn as the stubbornest Missouri mule. Now, I have your word that you're going to tell him?'

'Yes,' Tanya sighed, more frightened by the prospect than she cared to admit.

It was the longest night and day she had ever lived through. It was six-thirty the following evening and Jake hadn't arrived home yet. Tanya kept hoping he wouldn't come even though she knew it would only prolong the agony. Now that his father knew the truth Jake would find out whether she told him or not. She almost wished she had told J.D. to tell him if it weren't such a cowardly thing to do.

Three times she had changed her clothes, unable to decide what to wear. When she looked in the mirror, a hysterical bubble of laughter rose in her throat. She was wearing black with her amber-streaked hair coiled on top of her head. She looked as if she was going to a funeral; it felt as if it was her own.

She fussed with the powder, trying to hide the dark smudges under her eyes without success. She felt sick to her stomach and her hands were trembling like aspen leaves. The muscles were knotted at the back of her neck from the over-wrought state of her nerves.

At ten minutes before seven o'clock, she stepped into the hall, her knees barely supporting her as she walked down the hallway across the foyer to the secluded study on the opposite side of the house. J.D. was sitting behind the desk, his head resting against the back of the chair as he stared into space.

'He isn't home yet,' she spoke softly from the door, bringing his startled gaze around to her.

'No,' he sighed heavily. 'He isn't home. You might as well sit down. We can wait together.'

The leather-covered cushions seemed to close around her when she sat down, swallowing her up in its oversize proportions. It was a pleasant sensation marred by the ticking of the clock on the mantelpiece.

It was half past seven when they heard the sound of a car in the driveway. Tanya's fingers curled into the arm of the chair as she glanced fearfully at her father-in-law.

There was a grim smile on his face as he returned her look. 'It will all be over soon,' he said.

'Yes,' she whispered, 'it will all be over soon.'

Her eyelashes fluttered tightly down over her eyes at the sound of the front door shutting.

There was a sickening lurch in her stomach and she was terribly afraid she was going to be sick. She kept waiting for the sound of footsteps in the hall — Jake's footsteps. But the clock kept ticking in the silence.

After nearly ten minutes had gone by, J.D. began tapping a pencil impatiently on the desk top while glowering at the closed door. Tanya's nerves were stretched to screaming point. The knock on the door brought her to the edge of her chair.

'Come in,' J.D. called, motioning to Tanya to remain seated.

As the door swung open, the atmosphere threatened to stifle her. Jake looked so powerful in the slim-fitting brown trousers and the white short-sleeved shirt that was half unbuttoned to accentuate the bronzed colour of his skin, it took her breath away. His hair gleamed with rich brown tones, damp and slightly curling from a shower. But it was his face that Tanya stared at, so arrogantly carved and so disturbingly attractive.

'Sorry I'm late, Dad,' he said, without a hint of sincere apology in his voice as he moved through the doorway. 'I decided to freshen up f-first.' His gaze had moved from his father to Tanya, changing from indifferent blandness to glittering cold. His mouth snapped shut into a grim line as he glared at J.D. 'I thought you were alone. Excuse me.'

He pivoted sharply to leave, his rigid carriage

announcing his refusal to be in the same room with her.

'Come back in here!' J.D. barked.

'I'll come back when you're alone,' Jake retorted, the muscles in his arm rippling as he gripped the side of the door.

'You are not leaving,' his father declared in a tone that brooked no opposition. 'And Tanya is not leaving either.'

She saw the muscle twitching in Jake's tightly clenched jaw and knew the tight rein he held on his temper. The knowledge that he couldn't stand to be in her company was a physical pain in her heart.

'I don't mean to be disrespectful, Dad,' Jake declared. His back was still turned to his father as he spoke through gritted teeth. 'But this is none of your damned business.'

'I beg to differ with you, son,' J.D. answered with the same note of ominous softness in his voice. 'I have a stake in the future of my grandson, so that makes me involved.'

'If you're trying to act as a marriage counsellor, I suggest you have a talk with Tanya first,' Jake sneered, tossing a venomous look at Tanya, who cringed inwardly at the malevolence in his eyes.

'I already have — that's why I asked you here tonight. Now close that door and come in here and sit down.' She knew that only Jake's father could get away with ordering him around like that. No one else would dare that smouldering anger.

179

The door closed with a resounding slam as Jake turned on his heel and walked to the chair near Tanya's. He reclined his long length in it, looking amazingly relaxed, but she knew it was the watchful stillness of a jungle cat.

'Let's get this over with,' he muttered, glancing at the gold watch on his arm. 'I have a dinner date tonight.'

'With Sheila?' Tanya didn't realize she had spoken the question out aloud until the harshness of Jake's blue eyes bored into her.

'Do you care?' he jeered.

'That will be enough of that,' J.D. reprimanded. 'We aren't here to trade insults.'

Tanya had lowered her chin nearly into her chest, breaking free from Jake's look of scorn and contempt that slashed at her heart. She heard the click of a lighter and smelled the subsequent aroma of burning cigarette tobacco.

'Exactly why am I here?' Jake demanded, sending a cloud of smoke into the centre of the room. 'Are we supposed to be discussing the divorce settlement or what?' She felt the half-closed, hooded gaze piercing her flesh. 'Because if so, I want you to know that I won't give you one penny of alimony and I intend to fight you every inch of the way for custody of my son.'

The bitter vengeance in his voice brought Tanya to her feet, her hands twisting together like the knots in her stomach. How he despised her!

'Tanya,' J.D.'s gentle voice reached out to her, reassuring and warm, promising her all his support. Her beseeching gaze sought out the craggy features of the still handsome older man.

'I don't think I can do it,' she whispered as hot tears scalded her eyes.

'Tears,' Jake scoffed with cynical amusement. 'Now that is very touching!'

'Of course you can, Tanya.' J.D. sent a sharp, reproachful dart at his son. 'That is if my arrogant son will keep his mouth shut long enough to listen.'

'Why do you insist on butting into this?' Jake nearly exploded. 'You don't even know what's going on.'

'I know more than you do!' his father retorted just as angrily. 'And if you'll shut up and listen you might find out something, too!'

'Stop tearing at each other!' Tanya cried, unable to stand the angry bickering between father and son. 'I won't have you yelling at each other because of me!'

'You've been a strain on my relationship with my family since the first day I married you. Why should it suddenly be different now?' Jake's sarcasm lashed out at her with the fury of a cat-o'-nine-tails. But he didn't wait for her answer. 'Now tell whatever story it is you have to tell. I'm getting tired of all this melodramatic suspense.'

Tanya looked helplessly at the man behind the desk, praying that he would speak up and make the onerous explanation. But her father-in-law only nodded for her to go ahead.

'I don't know how to start,' she hedged weakly.

'For God's sake, just say whatever it is you're going to say so I can get the hell out of here!' Jake snarled, viciously stubbing his cigarette out in the ashtray beside the chair.

'You're not making it easy, Jake,' Tanya replied, sending him a slightly angry glance of her own.

'When have you ever made my life easy?' he asked coldly.

There was a moment of silence as her retaliatory anger faded at his harsh reminder of her own past treatment of him. She took a deep breath and wiped the tears from her cheek. Her feet put more distance between them as she stared down at her tightly knotted fingers.

'The other day wh-when we were talking,' she began quietly, 'you said you admired my honesty. I haven't been honest with you, Jake — in fact I've led you to believe something that isn't true at all.'

She glanced at him apprehensively, seeing his reaction to her statement. He was watching her, his gaze cold as he impatiently waited for her to continue.

'It's about John.' Her teeth bit into her lip to keep the choking sobs from rising out of her chest. The taste of blood mingled with her pain.

'What about John?' he prompted her.

From the corner of her eye she could see the grim, uncompromising line of his mouth. She forced herself to meet his gaze, unconsciously squaring her shoulders as she made the half turn towards him.

'He is not my son.'

The words had barely been spoken when Jake loomed to his feet, gliding across the distance separating them like an avenging angel. His hands closed over her soft upper arms, his fingers digging into the bone as he drew her up on tiptoe until she was inches away from his enraged face. Round amber eyes stared into his anger, mutely accepting his right to hold her so violently.

'What utter piece of nonsense is this? What are you saying?' he demanded, shaking her roughly. 'Are you trying to make me believe that John isn't my son?'

'No,' she murmured, the tears running down her cheeks again. 'He is your son. I've never lied about that.'

'Then what are you talking about?'

'John isn't my son. I'm not his mother,' Tanya repeated more forcefully.

'You're not making any sense.' His forehead drew together in a disbelieving frown. 'If you're not his mother, then who is?'

She swallowed the painful lump in her throat and lowered her gaze to the curling hairs on his chest. He was so near to her, yet so very far away.

'My sister,' she mumbled, gasping with pain as he suddenly increased the grip on her arms.

'That's a lie!' Jake snarled. 'I don't believe a word you're saying!'

'It's the truth. I swear it,' she whispered fervently.

'No!' he shouted, causing her to shrink away from him. He released her abruptly. 'I don't believe you.'

'She's telling you the truth, son,' J.D. said quietly, and Jake turned towards him.

'What do you know about this? Don't tell me you believe this wild tale?' he mocked savagely.

The older man didn't answer immediately, picking up a document from the desk and holding it out to Jake. 'I don't think you've seen this,' he said calmly.

Tanya waited with paralysed stillness as Jake frowned over the paper. She guessed it was John's birth certificate — her father-in-law had no doubt obtained a copy of it several years before. A suppressed anger remained in Jake's eyes as he turned to look at her.

'Deanna Carr is your sister?' he snapped.

The coiled hair on top of her head bobbed in a jerky movement of affirmation.

'Why?' he snarled. 'Why did you let me believe all these years that you were John's mother?'

'Because you were his father. You would have taken him away from me. I didn't have any family, no decent place to live, no means to support myself or John. I didn't stand a chance of him being awarded to me legally through the courts, not when Jake Lassiter was his father.'

'First,' Jake said, with deadly calm, 'I had to live with the fact that you'd borne my illegitimate son.' Bitter anger made his voice vibrate. 'Now you tell me his mother was some girl I don't even remember!'

The birth certificate was crunched into a tight ball in his hand. The room became filled with an oppressive silence that pounded as loudly as Tanya's heart. In the next instant the paper was hurled across the room.

'You ask too much!' his tight voice declared, every muscle in his body rippling with the violence and tension of the moment.

A tiny sob escaped as a moan from Tanya's lips. She couldn't face him any more, not after all the hurt she had caused him.

'I'm sorry, Jake,' she murmured numbly, whirling away from him to rush out of the study door.

CHAPTER TEN

'Tanya!'

Jake's angry voice called after her, but she didn't stop. Her steps quickened when she heard the sound of his in the hallway, following her. She couldn't stop, not even when his commanding voice called her name again.

'Tanya, come back here!'

Jake already despised her for rejecting his love. His loathing would have doubled after learning of the way she had used him for the last seven years. And she couldn't find it in her heart to blame him.

So intent on reaching the safety of her room was she, Tanya nearly ran into her mother-in-law, who had hurried into the hallway at the sound of her son's strident voice. Quickly she brushed past her, seeing the startled, questioning look on Julia's face with uncaring pain. Her mother-in-law's voice followed Tanya on the flight to her room.

'Jake, what's going on here? What's happened?' she demanded.

'Not now, Mother,' he brushed her aside impatiently.

'I want to know what's going on. I have a right to know what goes on in my own house!' Julia declared angrily.

'Let him be,' J.D.'s calming voice joined in.

'But I want to know —'

A hand was raised to shush her. 'I'll tell you all about it. Now where is John?'

'Out in the garden.'

Tanya heard the last as she opened her bedroom door and closed it quickly behind her, unconsciously turning the lock. An instant later she heard Jake's footsteps at the door and saw the jiggling of the doorknob.

'Open the door, Tanya!'

She cringed at the still angry tone. 'Please go away, Jake. Just go away.'

'Open this door or I swear I'll break it down!'

She hesitated for only a minute before reaching out with a trembling hand to unlock the door. The click sounded loudly in the sudden silence. As the knob turned in response to the sound, she moved swiftly away from the door, her eyes bright with unshed tears while she fought for the strength to make it through his inquisition. Silently she resolved not to cry nor attempt to gain his sympathy. She wasn't entitled to it, not after the way she had abused his trust.

He was in the room. Even with her back to him, she could feel his presence in the room before she heard the closing of the door. Breathing in deeply, she looked up at the ceiling and blinked away the tears in her eyes, while she waited for him to speak.

'Look at me, Tanya,' Jake ordered in a ruthless tone of tightly leashed anger.

Very slowly she turned around, not knowing how completely composed her rigidly held features made her appear. She stared into his glitteringly harsh eyes, an intense shade of blue against the bronze hue of his tanned skin.

'Can't this wait until tomorrow, Jake?' she asked, clasping her trembling hands tightly together so they wouldn't betray her. 'You'll be late for your dinner appointment.'

'The instant I left, you'd pack your suitcases and leave,' he snarled, stating what had only been a half-formed thought in her mind, and her cheeks coloured in admission. 'We'll finish this discussion right here and now.'

'I don't know what more I can tell you.' Her chin lifted instinctively. 'I can only say how terribly sorry and ashamed I am that I didn't tell you the truth sooner.'

'I'll bet you are,' Jake mocked, his lip curling with contempt. 'You've somehow managed to convince my father of the sincerity behind your actions, but you have yet to convince me.'

'Convince you of what?'

'Why you married me.'

'I married you because of John. I told you that,' she replied in a hurt voice. 'Once I made the mistake of telling you that he was your son and realized you weren't going to treat it lightly, I felt I had no choice. I loved him as if he *were* my own son.'

'The idea of being Mrs. Jake Lassiter didn't enter it at all?' he jeered. 'Not when you knew it would mean living in a beautiful home, being free of any financial worries, enjoying the status of a member of the Lassiter family, wearing clothes that you wouldn't even have dreamt of trying on before? That had no bearing on your decision?'

Pride gleamed brightly in her gold-flecked eyes. 'I won't pretend that I didn't know the Lassiters were a wealthy and respected family, because I did,' she answered calmly. 'But I can't make you believe me when I say that those things mattered only because of John. They were his birthright. He was entitled to them. I knew I never was.'

'It's funny the way it didn't stop you from using them for yourself,' he murmured sarcastically.

'If you want to brand me as a scheming, gold-digging tramp, I can't stop you, Jake.' She forced herself to meet the diamond sharpness of his gaze. 'I can only tell you that my concern was for John's future.'

Jake stared at her for a long moment, finally breaking away to shake his head in disgusted exasperation. 'I don't know why I believe you, but I do,' he muttered angrily.

The constriction of her throat made it impossible for Tanya to speak for a moment. 'Thank you,' she whispered tightly.

Running his fingers through his tobacco

brown hair, Jake turned and walked to the window, staring absently out at the gathering crimson dusk. His hands slid partially into the pockets of his trousers.

'I could accept you as John's mother. I could believe that. But to find out that she's really someone I don't remember —' There was a jerky, negative movement of his head to the side. 'I want to know about that night, Tanya.'

The grimness of his voice reached out and placed a cold hand on her heart.

'Oh, Jake,' she murmured in a weak protest at what he was asking.

'Did she — Did your sister tell you I was the father?' he persisted.

Tanya realized he was determined to know every bit of the story. 'Yes, she did.'

'Tell me what happened that night. Tell me everything you know,' he commanded harshly, not turning away from the window.

Her eyes lovingly caressed the back of his squared shoulders and the arrogant tilt of his head. She longed to rush over and put her arms about him and take away some of his pain. But Jake had asked her to inflict more. At this point she couldn't refuse him.

'Deanna and I went to the fair and the dance together. She was with some friends when you met me.' She began the explanation hesitantly, not knowing anywhere else to begin except at the beginning. 'I'm sure she wasn't around those first few times you asked me to dance. You were very handsome and charming. Every time you looked at me you seemed to steal my breath away. I'd never met anyone like you before.'

'Why did you run away from me?'

'It sounds foolish now,' Tanya sighed. 'You'd kissed me several times on the dance floor, but the last time — well it was different. It frightened me. It frightened me because of the way it made me feel. I wanted you to go on kissing me. All of those warm feelings of desire made me afraid so I ran.'

'I looked for you,' Jake said with a strange, far-away indifference in his voice. 'Where did you go?'

'I went to our car. Our parents had let us use their car and I went to it with the intention of leaving. But I couldn't go because Deanna wasn't with me. And I was beginning to feel silly for making such a production out of a kiss, so I came back — not right back, because I argued with myself for quite a while in the car park. It was probably a half an hour or more.' She breathed in deeply remembering the misery and confusion of those moments. 'When I came back, there was this boy I knew standing near the entrance. I asked him if he had seen Deanna and he told me she was over by the bar. I walked over there and saw her standing beside you.'

'Are you sure she was with me?' Jake asked sharply. 'Couldn't she have simply been standing next to me?'

'No,' she replied quietly, and swallowed the

191

lump in her throat. 'Dennis — the boy at the door — had followed me. He said, "Isn't that the guy who was giving you the rush a few minutes ago?" I don't remember if I answered him or not. Then he said, "You'd better warn your sister. Those Lassiters play fast and loose. If a girl isn't willing, they'll find one who is." '

Jake pivoted sharply around at that statement, his face angry and grim. 'Do you believe that?'

'Not so much any more,' Tanya shook her head quietly. 'At the time I think I did and more so later.'

'Which is why you despised me so much before,' he said coldly. 'When I wasn't successful in getting what I wanted from you, I used your sister. That's what you thought, wasn't it?' There was an expression of self-disgust on his face. 'How did you know for sure that your sister was with me?'

'About the time I decided to walk over to where the two of you were standing, some boy came up to ask Deanna to dance. You put your arm around her and told him hands off — she was private Lassiter stock.'

There was a heavy, almost groaning sigh from Jake as he turned swiftly towards the window.

Tanya wanted to stop, but she knew she had to go on. 'Later I managed to see Deanna alone. I tried to warn her about you, but she wouldn't listen to me. She told me she was old enough to know what she was doing and for me to go home. I did. It was nearly five o'clock in the morning when she came home. All she could talk about was that you were coming to see her the following weekend. Then you didn't come or call or write. Our parents were killed in a car crash a few weeks later, and after that she told me she was pregnant.'

'Why can't I remember?' His irritated muse was spoken aloud. He glanced over his shoulder with a narrowed gaze at Tanya. 'Did she look like you? Could I have confused her memory with yours?'

'She was dark, a brunette, and shorter than I am,' she answered quietly. 'You'd been drinking quite a bit when you were with me and you had a drink in your hand when I saw you with Deanna.'

A silence hushed the room, stretching out over long moments during which Tanya listened to the sound of her own breathing. Jake drew back the sheer curtains, leaning his hand against the window jamb as he watched John playing with a toy bulldozer among the rocks.

'Why,' he began at last, still staring out the window, 'did you agree to try to make our marriage work? Was that only for John's sake, too?'

'No.' Somehow she endured his darting cold glance. 'I agreed at first because you said if it didn't work then we would explore the alternatives of ending our marriage. To me that meant a divorce. I wanted that very much.'

'Why didn't you say so before?' Jake snapped savagely. 'Or was the taste of vengeance so strong that you wanted to bring me all the way to my knees?'

Tanya flinched. 'Seven years ago I would have answered "yes" to that. Today, a week ago, even a month ago, it wasn't true,' she murmured. 'Lately I thought we had a chance to have a good marriage, that you might regard me with some affection, or enough to understand why I lied to you in the beginning.'

'You underestimate your ability,' Jake laughed bitterly, walking away from the window in her general direction. A cigarette was taken from his pocket and placed in his mouth, the lighter viciously snapped to give flame.

Tanya closed her eyes for a brief moment. 'When you told me you loved me and why, all I wanted was to crawl into a hole and die rather than have you find out the way I'd deceived you.'

'Why did you bother to tell me at all? Or did Father force you into it?'

'He told me I had to tell you,' she admitted, lowering her gaze to her hands.

'You could have gone on letting me believe John was your son. Why didn't you?'

Unconsciously her gaze strayed to the bed. 'If I hadn't told you and became a real wife to you — a wife who took more than just kisses,' she glanced back at him, pallor robbing her face of colour as she watched him stub out the freshly lit cigarette, 'you would have learned anyway that I . . . I hadn't given birth to your son.'

Jake stared at her, his head tilted to one side almost as if he didn't understand what she said. Then he took the step that brought him nearer, his hands closing over her shoulders. His gaze held hers with burning intensity.

'Do you mean . . . Are you telling me that. . . .' Then he groaned as he read the answer in her face. With a convulsive movement he drew her against his chest, burying his face in the coiled knot of her tawny hair.

And she clung to him, hopelessly praying that he would never let her go, that he would hold her like this for ever. She felt his mouth moving in a rough caress over her hair as he whispered her name.

'I wish you could forgive me,' she murmured, her heart singing a bittersweet melody. 'I love you so very much, darling.'

'Why? Because of John?' he demanded. 'You still want him?'

'I love John,' she admitted, understanding his reason for doubting the sincerity of her love. 'But my love for you is separate from him. I know you can't forgive me for deceiving you about him. But I love you, Jake.'

'No, no,' he protested savagely, dragging his head away from her. 'I'm the one who needs forgiveness, for what I did to you and your sister.'

'I'm not bitter about it any more.' Her hands tenaciously gripped his waist, refusing to let him push her aside.

'But it's there, between us. We can't pretend it didn't happen.' He stared down at her coldly, the muscle in his jaw twitching in his fight for control. 'I love you, Tanya, maybe more now that I realize what you sacrificed for my son.'

'My darling,' her fingers lightly touched his cheek, 'isn't that important? That we love each other?'

'Dammit, don't you understand?' Angrily he brushed her hand away. 'The blankness of that night haunts me. I don't know why I expect you to believe me, but I've never taken a woman who didn't already know the score. It was bad enough thinking I'd taken you in a night of drunkenness. The only thing I thought about that night was you. I don't remember looking at anyone else.'

His torment reached out to touch her trembling body. Tanya felt his anguish as if it were her own. All the love that burned within her was shining in the eyes that looked into his. The hands left her shoulders as he turned away, making a small gesturing shrug of helplessness.

'Do you have a picture of her?' he asked in a more subdued tone. 'Maybe if I saw it I could remember.'

'In my wallet.' Her handbag was on the dresser. Taking out the leather wallet, Tanya hurriedly flipped through the photographs to Deanna's. She handed it to Jake. He stared at it for a long moment, then shook his head.

'It's vaguely familiar,' he muttered, handing it back to her, 'but she has your smile.'

She started to put it back in her bag as his hand reached out to close over her wrist.

'Wait a minute!' he ordered sharply. He looked at it again, then at Tanya.

'Do you recognize her?' she breathed slowly.

'Think carefully,' he said, his eyes watching her closely. 'Did she say that it was me she was with that night? I mean me specifically, my name.'

'I guess so,' she shook her head in confusion. 'What are you getting at?'

'I'm asking you if she said she was with Jake Lassiter, or did you assume she was?'

'I don't remember. I was hurt and bitter. I didn't want to talk about you.'

'Is it possible she called me Jamie?'

'Jamie is your brother,' Tanya frowned. 'Why would she call you that?'

'Because my brother was with me that night. I vaguely remember that we didn't go back to the hotel together, but I imagined it was because I was with you.'

'But I saw you with Deanna!'

'Was there anyone else with us?'

'I can't remember,' she admitted.

'I know he met a girl there, but I was so wrapped up in finding you that I can't say whether she was fat or thin or short or bald,' he grumbled. 'Jamie introduced her to me.'

'Jake,' she spoke hesitantly, her own mind racing now with doubts, 'where was Jamie going the night he was killed?'

'I don't know. I think he had a date somewhere north of Springfield.' He shook his head, then stopped to stare at Tanya.

'When was he killed? Not the time, but the day.'

'Saturday.' His face began to clear. 'The weekend after the dance when I was supposed to have seen Deanna. It was Jamie!' Jake declared vehemently.

'When she told me she was pregnant, all I asked was whether the father was that Lassiter man she met at the dance. Of course she said yes, and we never mentioned a name again.' The pieces were beginning to fall into place. 'When John was born, Deanna was so ill that I was the one who gave them the information on the birth certificate. Your name. And all these years I blamed you,' she said in a horrified whisper. 'Oh, Jake, I'm sorry.'

'I'm not,' he sighed heavily. 'We can't be sure it was Jamie.'

'But, darling, we can't be sure it wasn't,' Tanya smiled. 'We do know that John is a Lassiter and your mother has shown me baby pictures of you and your brother. His resemblance to Jamie is re-markable.'

'His car was wrecked between here and Sadalia. I'd like to believe he was going to see Deanna. Maybe they did fall in love that night. I'd like to believe that,' Jake murmured, a rueful smile curving his mouth. 'If for no other reason than to assuage my conscience.'

'It's not so hard to believe. I think I fell in love with you that night, for a little while at least,' she admitted.

He drew her gently in his arms, holding her tenderly against his chest. 'I wonder what would have happened if you'd told me the truth seven years ago,' he murmured.

'I don't think we'll ever know,' she sighed, but it was a happy sigh.

'I love you, Tanya, my sweet, honest wife. I think I would have loved you anyway.' A tantalizing kiss touched her mouth. 'We might possibly have discovered the truth about Jamie and Deanna then and not had any of the bitterness and hostility we lived through.'

'I like to think,' she whispered, inching closer in his arms, 'that this has made our love stronger because it was born and survived where it had no right to, don't you?'

His answer was by deed, not words.

We hope you have enjoyed this Large Print book. Other G.K. Hall & Co. or Chivers Press Large Print books are available at your library or directly from the publishers.

For more information about current and up-coming titles, please call or write, without obligation, to:

G.K. Hall & Co.
P.O. Box 159
Thorndike, Maine 04986 USA
Tel. (800) 223-1244

OR

Chivers Press Limited
Windsor Bridge Road
Bath BA2 3AX
England
Tel. (0225) 335336

All our Large Print titles are designed for easy reading, and all our books are made to last.